Briefly Yours

An Erotic Romance

Madison Martin

Briefly Yours

Copyright © 2008 by Madison Martin

1

Heat surged through every inch of Ava Parker's body, and she squeezed her eyes tight while a wave of sensation overtook her. She braced her back against the wall and stifled a long, ragged moan. Her breath came in soft pants, and every muscle went limp, her legs threatening to give out beneath her. She fantasized about stripping her pantyhose off before sweat ran down her thigh.

Come on, now. Don't panic. You can do this.

It wasn't every morning she met with the Skiv-Ease International Board of Directors, and no matter how hard she'd worked the last few weeks to prepare the beginnings of the men's Valentine's Day underwear line, she couldn't calm down.

The CEO's assistant opened the conference room door and gave Ava a wide, warm smile. "They're ready for you, Ms. Parker."

Ava managed one deep breath, despite her pounding heart. "Thanks, Heather."

This is it. Don't blow it.

She clutched her large black portfolio in one hand, and felt her French twist with the other to make sure no strands had escaped. She smoothed down the skirt of her best black suit, cleared her throat, and strode into the conference room.

The nitty-gritty of the business went on in here, and from the rumors floating around the company the past few months, the nitty-gritty wasn't going too well.

Ava's eyes roamed from Marshall Matheson to Colin Sheppard, to Skiv-Ease International's CEO, Thomas Fielding. The guy to the right...she stifled another wave of panic. Nobody told her she'd be putting on a performance for *him* today, too.

He wore a hip designer suit and his dark brown hair in a trendy cut, but his killer smile would get him noticed if he were dressed in a potato sack. During the past two weeks she'd caught an occasional glimpse of him in the lobby, and once, she'd seen him walking outside on Melrose Avenue, laughing with another exec on their way back from lunch. The center of attention with everyone around him, he moved like he had all the time in the world.

She'd refused to act ridiculous like every other female in the company, and scoffed at their giggles and whispers while they took bets about the woman most likely to get "The New Guy" into bed. Some thoughtful person had stuck a copy of the final list they'd come up with in her inbox. At the very bottom, voted least likely to end up in the sack with Mr. Wonderful, was Ava Parker. She'd crumpled it up and tossed it into the recycle bin with a grimace. Part of her didn't blame her coworkers. After all, she wasn't bound to get a reputation as the company seductress designing granny panties.

Fielding stood and adjusted his jacket. "Good afternoon, Ms. Parker. You know Mr. Matheson and Mr. Sheppard." Fielding turned to Mr. Wonderful. "May I introduce Justin Barrett. Mr. Barrett will be overseeing the financial aspects of this year's Cupid's Beau Line."

Mr. Barrett stood to his impressive full height...six feet? Six one? He extended his hand, firm and gentle all at once when it closed over hers. "Ms. Parker." A deep and masculine voice accompanied a smile that made all the blood rush to her face.

When his confident, sparkling brown eyes met hers, Ava's mouth went dry. She tore her gaze away and muttered, "Nice to, uh…meet you." She wished she had something to wipe her clammy hands on. *Get a grip, Ava.* Since when did the sight of an attractive guy make her lose her concentration?

With renewed focus, she looked up at the execs and smiled. "Well, let's get right to work, shall we?"

The four men settled expectantly in their chairs, waiting for her to wow them. If she didn't know better she'd think Mr. Wonderful just checked her out. Feeling more than a little self-conscious, she opened her portfolio, and propped ten designs down on an easel. Her sketches of men's underwear were displayed before them: five pairs of boxers and five briefs, each with its own special design she imagined any woman would love her guy to wear. And since she couldn't remember the last time she'd seen a man in or out of his underwear, that's all she'd been doing: imagining.

She cleared her throat. "Gentlemen, may I present…my concepts for next year's Cupid's Beau Men's Valentine's Day line." She stepped aside so they could see the easel.

Out of the corner of her eye she caught Mr. Matheson nodding. Mr. Wonderful looked on, interested.

Conjuring up bravado, she held her hand out, presenting the first sketch. "These briefs are all about using flattering lines, but using a modern, cutting edge design at the same time. See how this first pair cuts just below the hip. I've given each pair in the line a special Valentine element." She pointed to lettering on the upper right side. "This one reads, 'Be Mine.'" Her hand moved to the waistband. "The dark red stitching around the elastic adds an extra little flair, and contrasts with the white fabric."

She glanced over and caught Thomas Fielding furrowing his brow. "Do you have any other sayings on there?" he asked.

"Oh, um…yes. There's plenty of room for longer sayings. No limit to that," Ava replied.

The exec nodded and scribbled down some notes.

She took a deep breath and drew their attention to the next sketch of a pair of red boxers. "These are designed to ride low on the hips, with a comfortable fit through the…um, through the rear…and the heart on the front not only adds a nice Valentine's touch, but also doubles as a single-packet condom pouch…"

Despite the flush burning her cheeks, she looked up and tried to find someone to make eye contact with. *That's what you're supposed to do while speaking in public.* Problem was, while the other three of them focused solely on the sketches, Mr. Barrett refused to look away from her. She cleared her throat and bit back a cough. "Any…any questions so far?"

Fielding's eyes narrowed and he scribbled a note on the yellow legal pad in front of him. "Can you summarize why you chose the color scheme you did?"

"Of course." That was a no-brainer. She'd spent the better part of a week toying with a scheme that worked. "Since the line is geared for the holiday, I felt the use of bright colors was important, so I used a consistent scheme throughout. Bold, but classy and simple."

Her voice trailed off and she held her breath, waiting for some sort of response. She fantasized about having had time to sew some mock-ups to prove the designs would look even better in 3-D than on paper.

After a tense moment of silence, someone finally spoke.

Matheson's gray eyes bored into hers. "Throw a thong or two in the line."

"At least two," Sheppard countered, clicking a ballpoint pen in and out. "Last year's demand was huge. We should offer a wide choice."

Ava gulped. *Thongs?* As if studying how best to flatter the male crotch with a pair of briefs hadn't stretched the limits of her imagination already.

Fielding cleared his throat and looked down his horn-rimmed glasses. "Barrett, get me a cost analysis for nylon. Thirty-thousand units…" He looked over at Justin, an expectant look on his face. "Aren't you going to write that down?"

Justin folded his arms across his chest, a confident smile on his face. "I've got it covered."

"Oh, no, Mr. Fielding." Ava's heart sank. "Not nylon. Microfiber for the briefs. And the highest quality silk for the boxers."

"And the highest expense," Justin Barrett pointed out.

Ava stiffened her shoulders and shot him a defensive glare. "That fabric is the core of my Conservo-Skiv-Ease line. Judging by sales last year…"

Justin cut her off. "I'm well aware of the profit last year from your Conservo line." His brown eyes met hers and he gave her a mischievous look that said he saw right through her.

She stiffened her spine and refused to let him faze her. "Then you realize the numbers speak for themselves. The Conservo line made…"

"I know exactly how much your line made last year," Justin interrupted. "I also know that the men's Valentine's Day items are purchased as novelties. The concept matters…not the execution. They won't be worn more than once, anyway. No man will care what they're made of." He relaxed against the back of the chair and crossed his legs at the ankles, hands behind his head.

Fielding tapped a pen on the table, a questioning look on his face.

She struggled to draw in a breath, trying not to let Mr. Barrett's easy, confident manner irritate her when her life's work was on the line. "Let's not forget that in most cases women will be buying these for men, and to them, the material we use is of the utmost importance. Last quarter we sold more of my microfiber bras than the cotton and synthetics combined." She found herself getting impatient. Justin might be a man, but she figured she'd learned more about men's underwear the past few weeks than he'd learned his entire life. "Besides…research shows that men like…uh…the softest thing they can get against their… um…their…"

His eyebrows shot up and he looked at her with an amused look on his face, like he couldn't wait to hear how she'd dig herself out of this one.

Her gaze darted toward the floor, then back up at him. "You get the picture," she murmured. She bit her lower lip.

"I think I'm beginning to." His twinkling brown eyes stared and challenged her. "I take it you've done extensive research on the topic?"

She folded her arms across her chest. She supposed he'd asked a valid question. If he knew her women's Conservo line, he knew that sexy men's underwear was the furthest thing from her usual work. But how dare he suggest she hadn't done her homework, when she'd been slaving away on this topic every spare second?

She gathered the last bit of confidence she could muster and held her head up high. "Trust me. I've done plenty of research." Her pulse raced. Since when did some financial guy decide which fabrics she could use? "How can you think anyone would want nylon boxers if there are better options?"

Justin stood up and came out from behind the table. He stuffed his hands into his pockets and paced for a few steps. "What other options did you have in mind?"

A rush of excitement coursed through her. If she could make them as enthusiastic as she was about her future plans, her work would be done. She had no choice but to strip her black blazer off. She grabbed a bit of her white silk blouse and thrust it toward him. "Feel this."

Justin's eyes met hers. They never left as he took the bit of silk in his hands, and brushed his fingers across the front of her blouse. A little jolt of electricity shot through her, and she tried to forget the fact that his touch made her insides melt.

Justin mused. "Not bad. But…" He gave her a look like he could one-up her little trick, and then reached down inside his pants and pulled out some fabric from his boxers. "Feel *this*." He swiveled his hip, inviting her to touch.

Without thinking, she grabbed a handful of fabric, letting her fingers slide against the soft, slick material.

He grinned. "Nice, huh?"

She had to admit the fabric was soft against her fingers. She furrowed her brow. "This is synthetic?"

His eyes met hers. "Yup."

She pulled her hand away. "I don't believe…"

Justin yelped.

What the…? She looked down to find her silver watch caught in his underwear, and she'd yanked something she shouldn't have. She panicked trying to pull away and ended up pulling more material with it instead.

"Hold on." Justin's hand covered hers to stop her from doing more damage.

"Sorry," she murmured, her face growing hot. The last thing she wanted was to end up with her hand stuck in his crotch. "Here, let me…"

"I can handle it…"

She glanced up and found a horrified look on Fielding's face, and wished she could sink into the floor.

They wrestled over the watch, until a loud ripping sound reverberated through the room.

She gasped, and looked down to discover that Justin's boxers now had a nice hole in them. "Uh…sorry."

He grinned at her.

"If you two are finished." Fielding's voice echoed through the huge conference room.

Ava raised her head and found the Board staring at Justin and her like they'd both lost their minds. She cleared her throat and whispered,

"Um, yes. Quite finished."

Justin tucked his boxers back in and readjusted his pants. "Yep," he said, looking chagrined.

"Good!" Fielding boomed, shuffling the pile of paperwork in front of him. He glanced up at Ava through his bifocals. "Ms. Parker, thank you for…enlightening us on the Cupid's Beau line." He stood and adjusted his tie. "Now if you'll excuse us, we'll get back to business."

Gathering up the last remnants of her dignity, she pursed her lips and gathered up her designs. "Of course."

The board members filed out of the conference room, leaving her to clean up her presentation. If there was one thing she took seriously, it was her work, and she'd just made a complete fool of herself.

Ava trudged down the hall toward her office, barely picking her heels up off the floor. All that work…and they hated it. Tears came to her eyes. "Back to business" probably meant figuring out how to tell her they were taking Cupid's Beau away from her. Then again, this wasn't completely her fault. What were they thinking, placing her in charge of creating this line? Everyone knew she designed the most conservative underwear on the planet. Sure, her department had been the most successful one in the company last year, but she specialized in comfort, not sex appeal.

She turned to find Leslie Ferguson and Derek DeMarco of the Spicy Hot Lingerie line behind her.

"Hey, Ava," Leslie teased. "I tried on your Lift-O-Bra the other night. It's got so much under wire I can hang all my suits on it."

Ava grimaced without looking back. The creators of ultra-sexy women's lingerie, Derek and Leslie loved nothing better than to torture Ava every chance they got. They thrived on coming into her office and attacking her mannequins. They'd strip off their girdles, robes, or new bras, then put them on and prance down the hallway laughing for everyone in the company to see.

"P.S." Derek chimed in. "Love your new Girdle-Skiv-E. My grandmother wouldn't be caught dead without it!"

Ava rolled her eyes, oh-so-happy to be the butt of their jokes. She picked up the pace while she headed down the hallway.

"Wait up, Ava! Hey! How'd the meeting for Cupid's Beau go?" Leslie called after her.

Ava clutched her portfolio more tightly against her chest and ignored them.

"Hey, we're not laughing at you! We're laughing *with* you," Derek laughed, nudging Ava's shoulder while he and Leslie walked past.

Ava grimaced when they almost made her drop her portfolio. *If they're so smart, how come my line's the only one that turned a profit last year?*

Heather brushed past carrying a stack of white full-body slips over one arm. "Don't listen to a word they say," she said. "They're just jealous. Since the minute Andrea left, everyone's been clawing all over each other to get Cupid's Beau."

"Thanks." Ava sighed, grateful to have someone on her side. She managed the slightest hint of a smile despite her watery eyes. Sure, everyone might want to take over the line, but did they want the pressure that came along with it?

Rumor had it that Andrea Chatsworth was one pair of briefs away from finishing the all-important Valentine's Day line before her nervous breakdown. She'd destroyed every design she'd created, leaving Ava without so much as a starting point.

Everyone knew how much pressure came with this line. Almost a quarter of the company's profits for the year came from it, and when Ava had been ordered to take over, she hadn't been given the slightest hint of what to do. Although she'd done her best, who was she kidding? If that meeting was any indication, she hadn't been up to the task.

"Barrett, what are you thinking? Can Parker pull this off?" Fielding took a sip of wine over lunch on the patio at Marino's Restaurant on Melrose. He pushed his glasses further up his nose and waited with an expectant look on his face for Justin to answer.

"We've got a lot riding on her if we let her take this on," Fielding continued. "This company has taken a lot out of me. I've thought about selling it off piece by piece, but something tells me to give it one more shot. I'm too close to it and I can't decide what's best. I need your help."

Justin watched the lunchtime crowd perusing the shops and wolfed down another bite of chicken cacciatore. No question about it: the woman had done her homework, and despite her fabric choices, he liked the plans she had for Cupid's Beau. Considering the Conservo-Skiv-Ease line was the only one to make it out of the red last year, she had to be doing something right. Hearing her out was the least he could do. He wouldn't exactly consider it a chore taking a meeting with her. Maybe he'd find out if she always wore her dark brown hair up in a twist. Did she let it fall loose around her face every now and then? Watching those sexy little dimples in her cheeks while she spoke drove him crazy that morning. And no guy stood a chance looking into those green eyes.

Justin cleared his throat and dug his fork into the pasta. "I'll need to do further research. Weigh the cost versus benefit. I have more questions for Ms. Parker."

Fielding didn't have to know that his further research included finding out what she wore underneath that conservative black business suit. Did she know how turned on a guy could get when a woman wore those? The sight of her long, sexy legs in black stockings was enough to do him in. And did she actually wear the granny underwear she designed? Or was that all for show, and underneath she had on some sexy little bikini? Not that it mattered one way or the other. Whatever her personal

Skiv-Ease attire consisted of, he planned on getting her out of it as soon as possible.

He thought about how easily her cheeks flushed, her shy reaction to her own work, and knew it would take more than a flash of his smile to get her right where he wanted her.

Later, at her desk, Ava popped two painkillers and washed them down with a glass of water. She let every bit of air out of her lungs with an exhausted sigh. She'd spent the afternoon putting the finishing touches on a new minimizing bra, trying not to think about the morning's events. No one had come in to can her, but she hadn't received one word from the Board, either. She'd heard they'd been in closed-door meetings all afternoon with Mr. Barrett.

She stared out the window. Once again, it had gotten dark and she realized she'd been inside the entire day. Now nightlife perked up in restaurants and the neighboring theaters on Melrose Avenue. More events she'd miss.

If they took the Cupid's Beau away from her, she'd just have to go right back to what she did best. Straightening her back, she cleared some room on her desk by pushing aside a pile of flesh-colored panties, and prepared to put in a few more hours of work before going home for the night. She searched through some files on her computer, digging around for something she'd started working on yesterday.

A knock on the door broke her concentration. She jumped. It was after eight, and normally everyone had gone home by now. She looked up to find Justin Barrett leaning against her door, holding his jacket over his shoulder with one finger. Her gaze flew down to the tanned masculine flesh revealed by one more button of his shirt undone than she remembered that morning. Her heart jumped a little at the sight. She blinked, feeling a hot flush creep through her. "May I help you?"

"Mind if I come in for a minute?" Before she could answer, he strode into her office like he owned the place.

"Do I have a choice?"

She caught him checking out her office.

"I think you'll like what I have to say."

She moved a pile of notebooks from her desk to the small glass table behind her before she looked back up at him. "And what's that? I have an hour to clean out my desk?" she asked dryly.

He laughed. "No, they liked your line. They're giving you a shot."

Relief flooded through her. "You're kidding."

"They liked what you've got so far and they want to see more." He shrugged, setting his jacket over her green leather couch. "With the thongs, of course." His eyes searched hers. "You look shocked."

"I didn't think my presentation came off too well."

"Why? It was right on the money, and they know they can rely on you. It's no secret the company's not in great shape, is it?"

"No."

"It's sink or swim time. You're Skiv-Ease's best shot." He gave her a smile. "The future of the company is riding on you."

"No pressure or anything." She rose to her feet, her heart sinking with the reminder.

"Come on. You were the picture of creativity today. You can do it."

"Thanks for the vote of confidence, but…" She pictured everyone's job on the line. Including hers. The thought made her shudder.

"You don't look like a woman who'd turn down a challenge." His eyes twinkled. "Or have a problem living up to it."

She drew her lower lip into her mouth. He had that right.

"Anyway, I came in here because there are a few financial aspects I need to discuss with you."

She fumbled through some papers on her desk. "I thought we already did that."

"We barely scratched the surface. I have some more questions."

She raised one eyebrow. "I thought I made it clear where I stand on the fabric issue."

His eyes never left hers. "Aw, come on now…I'm an open-minded guy. You can do the same for me, right?"

No wonder everyone fell at his feet. He did know how to give someone his entire focus, like the object of his attention was the most important person he'd ever known. How could anyone look in his spell-binding brown eyes and tell him no?

His gaze roamed over two of the female mannequins in her office. Both of them were dressed in garments from her Conservo-Skiv-Ease line. One wore a stark white pair of briefs, the other a flesh-colored girdle.

He turned and gave Ava the once-over.

She panicked looked down at herself. *Did I spill something on my blouse at lunch?*

He ran one hand through his short dark hair and sat on the corner of her desk. The full lips of his beautiful mouth curved into a warm, genuine smile, and he casually stuffed one hand in the pocket of his black dress pants, jingling a set of keys inside. "Your Conservo-Skiv-Ease line is a legend around here."

"Sure, it is," she said sarcastically. "Everyone loves buying my items for their grandmas, right?" She nodded disapprovingly toward his bum planted on the edge of her desk. Great view or not, she didn't want it there. "Mr. Barrett, do you mind?"

With a deep, sexy laugh, he jumped off the desk. "Listen, I have a lot of respect for your work."

She ignored the teasing sparkle in his velvet brown eyes and grimaced. *I'll just bet you do.* Somehow she doubted anything in her line was the kind of garment he'd buy for the women in his life.

"I know how important the fabric you use is," he murmured. He moved closer, the clean, masculine smell of him invading her senses.

"No, I don't think you do."

His voice was low and quiet, his eyes looking directly into hers. "I know that your line is meant to be comfortable. However…" He leaned even closer, like he was revealing a huge secret. "What I don't think you're getting here…is that the Cupid's Beau line is meant to be taken *off*."

Ava gulped. He moved even closer to her, and she wished she could get up the nerve to kick Mr. Insolent out of her office. He stood way too close for comfort and she thought about backing away. She couldn't make herself do it. "I don't…I don't care who takes it off or *when* they take it off," she stammered. "That's not the point. I'm not going to put my name on something that isn't up to par."

He nodded, pondering. "I can respect that."

Her eyes roamed over his five o'clock shadow…eight o'clock shadow? She wondered if his face would be rough to her touch. "I don't think you care about up to par, though, do you?" she murmured. "I think you just care about the money."

She watched the mesmerizing sight of his mouth moving, wondering what it would be like to kiss him. Something told her it would be a most enjoyable experience.

He cocked his head. "Well?"

She realized she'd been so busy staring at his mouth she hadn't heard a word that just came out of it. "Well, what?"

He nodded toward her, impatient. "Yes or no?"

"I'm sorry, I didn't…"

"Since you seem to think I only care about money, why don't you meet me at Morton's tomorrow night for drinks so I can prove otherwise?"

No way. She wasn't meeting him for work or anything else tomorrow night. "No, I don't think that's such a good…"

He shrugged and grinned at her. "It's the least you can do for ripping my shorts."

His dark eyes shone, focused on her alone. The way he looked at her…moving in closer, invading her space and her senses, drove her crazy. Her heart pounded and her breath caught in her throat. Was Justin Barrett about to kiss her?

2

Ava blinked hard and awkwardly smoothed her skirt when Justin took a step back from her.

He stuffed his hands in his pockets and strolled toward her couch. "It would help with my cost analysis if I had a mock-up of a few of your designs."

Why did I think he was going to kiss me? She remembered her position on the "most likely to do the horizontal hula with the hottie" list. Dead last.

Grimacing, she cleared her throat and decided to distract herself by cleaning off her desk. "Fine. I'll have those mock-ups to you by tomorrow, Mr. Barrett."

He gave her a look that said that impressed him. "That's a quick turnaround."

"Well, that's me." She gave a nervous laugh and picked up a small pile of oversized strapless bras. "No time to waste."

She shoved the bras in the cabinet behind her, glanced up, and did a double take. She'd neglected to notice that someone had dressed her favorite mannequin in a sleazy, see-through red teddy. She frowned and made a mental note to keep her office locked when she wasn't there. Derek and Leslie would hear about this later.

She stripped off the offensive garment and looked up to find Justin staring at the teddy in her hands.

He scratched his forehead. "I kind of like that one."

She shot him a look. He *would.* She tossed the teddy in the trash bin in the corner of her office and swiped her hands together. "Mr. Barrett, why can't we talk about whatever business you need to discuss tomorrow during the day?"

"Let's see…" Rubbing his chin while he mused, he paced from the couch to the mannequins near the window, and back again. "I've got an eight a.m. breakfast, a ten, an eleven, lunch in the Valley, and back to back meetings all afternoon." He stopped, sprawling out on her couch with a deep sigh. "Only opening I've got is drinks." He looked up at her, an expectant look in his eyes while he mulled over his plan. "Of course, eight is getting late." His eyes brightened. "Might work better if we have dinner along with those drinks."

One look at his irresistible smile and she clued in to his ultimate talent: getting whatever he wanted from people. And most likely making them think he was doing them a favor in the process. If she didn't watch it, he'd use his charm on her, and next thing she knew her line would consist of cheesy fabric in some cheap lingerie department. Her shoulders stiffened. *Let him try.* It would take more than a few winks and drinks from him to destroy her life's work. In the meantime, dinner at Morton's would be more interesting than her usual: a frozen diet package of something or other tossed in the microwave.

She sighed and sat back down at her desk. "If that's what it'll take to get you off my couch…fine. Morton's at eight." She folded a T-back bra and prepared to shove it in the cabinet.

"Great. I'll look forward to it." Watching her with a triumphant smile, he grabbed his jacket and strolled out of her office.

Ava heaved out a helpless sigh.

Gasping for breath, Ava tossed three pairs of men's skivvies on the cherry wood bar at Morton's the next night. Through the dark ambience of the restaurant, the bartender shot her a smile. She shoved the mock-ups toward Justin and then sat down beside him on one of the barstools.

Justin turned toward her with a grin, an unfinished drink in his hand. He picked up a pair of the underwear and looked it over. "Hey. Wow. They're done."

She took a deep gulp of air. "Fielding called me into his office right before I was supposed to leave and I had to run over here in these..." She glanced down at her three-inch pumps.

She figured he took that as an invitation to let his gaze drift down her body to her heels. He smiled, looking sexier than ever in a light blue dress shirt and a perfectly matched silk tie. How could he look that good after a long day of work? Meanwhile, she could feel her French twist about to fall out, and her strenuous efforts to get here on time were making her start to sweat.

She gingerly picked up the mock-ups. "Sorry, I'm not usually late..."

He glanced at his watch. "I just got here. And two minutes isn't exactly..."

She fumbled in her purse for her compact to check out the damage in the little mirror. "Late is late...but the mock-ups are done. As per your request."

He picked up one of the thongs and examined it. "You work fast."

She opened the compact inside her purse and snuck a look at herself. She tucked a few loose strands of hair behind her ears. "I always meet my deadlines, Mr. Barrett."

He grinned. "I prefer Justin." He loosened his tie a little and relaxed. "After six p.m., anyway."

She snapped the compact shut and tried not to be drawn in by the fascinating male presence beside her.

"You know...I didn't mean you had to stress yourself out for this..."

Not stress? Of course she had to stress. It was her middle name. She pursed her lips. "Stress goes with the territory, Mr. Barrett."

"You all right?"

"Fine." About to die of heatstroke, she removed her blazer and placed it on the back of the chair. He motioned toward the bartender, and before she knew it, a big glass of ice water appeared on the bar.

Justin pushed it toward her. "Here, have at it."

"Thanks," she said, taking a gulp of cold water. If she didn't know better, she'd think he just gave her cleavage a discreet look. She self-consciously shifted in her chair.

He grabbed the red thong. "What is this one made out of?"

"The finest microfiber," she replied.

"Looks expensive."

She wrapped her hands around the water glass. "Quality is expensive."

"Listen, while you were stitching your fingers to the bone, I did a little work, myself."

Ava turned to find two extremely tall women dressed in short skirts and high heels rushing up to the bar. "Justin!" they cried.

He turned to them. "Hey, Miranda. Kylie. How's it going?" He introduced them to Ava, but they barely gave her a glance before fawning over Justin again.

"What are you doing here, Jus?" Kylie asked.

"Shopping, from the looks of it," Miranda giggled, staring at the thong. She gave Justin the once over. "Those will look good on you."

Justin smiled proudly at Ava. "Yeah."

Kylie traced her finger down his shoulder and gave him a seductive look. "Good luck. We'll see you around." They sauntered toward the restaurant section together.

"Anyway," Justin said, turning his full attention to Ava, "the fact is…there's a huge cost difference between the nylon and…other fabrics."

"Are those your…friends?" Ava asked casually. *Not that it's any of my business.*

"Huh? No. They just hang out here a lot. So do I. You know what I mean about the cost differences, right?"

He does know they both want to jump his bones, right? Then again, maybe they already had. Together. She shuddered, but then stiffened her shoulders. He could be into ménage à trois or anything else for all she cared. She ignored the remote possibility that she might be jealous.

"Ava?"

She shook her head, jolting back to reality. "Oh, yeah. I don't think about costs much, or let them keep me from designing something that might work. What other fabrics are we talking about?" she asked.

"Uh…" He grinned. "For example…what do you call that fabric?" He snapped his fingers. "It's like satin…but it's not satin?"

"Sateen?"

"Yeah, that's it. What kind of quality is that?"

"It depends," she murmured. One look at his suit and she knew the guy took pride in dressing well, but could she really fault him for not knowing one fabric from another? He was a consultant, here to save the company. Knowing fabrics was her job. And maybe it was her job to clearly demonstrate her point. She quickly formulated a plan.

"I want you," she blurted out. She squeezed her eyes shut and cringed when the words registered. *Did that really just come out of my mouth?*

Justin's eyebrows raised and he gave out a subtle laugh. "Hmm…I like the sound of that."

Her face flushed. "I mean...I want you to *come* with me."

He nearly choked on his drink. "Even better."

"I mean…come with me…on a hands-on research trip," she finished quickly.

Justin's eyes brightened. "Hands on? Now that sounds interesting."

She rolled her eyes. "What I'm trying to say is…I want to show you some real stores with the kind of garments I'm going for. If I show you some successful lines, I can convince you that Cupid's Beau can only succeed with the highest quality materials. I want a chance to prove my point."

He shrugged. "Great. I want a chance to prove mine."

"So…" She looked up, barely letting her eyes meet his. "How do we do this?"

"I'll come pick you up tomorrow and we'll go at it."

She gulped and nearly knocked her glass over. Collecting her wits, she asked in the calmest voice she could muster, "Um…go at it?"

"Check out some stores and execute this plan of yours?"

She lowered her eyes. "Oh, right," she said softly.

He finished his drink and pushed the glass aside on the bar. "How about I pick you up at ten?"

"Sharp."

"Great. I just need one thing. Your address."

"Oh, yeah." She dug a business card out of her purse, scribbled her address on it and handed it to him.

Justin's cell rang as he tucked her card in his wallet.

She furrowed her brow. She grew nervous thinking it might be Fielding or another boss. "Aren't you going to get that?"

"No." Unconcerned, he turned the phone off without seeing who it was, and shot her a devilish smile. "Now...how about dinner?"

"Why can't you come to Vegas?"

Morning sunlight poured into Ava's bedroom. Holding the phone in the crook of her neck, she listened to the pleas of her friend Charlotte while tossing some fabric samples into her purse. "I have to stop the Cupid's Beau line from turning into cheesy discount store fodder. It's an emergency."

Dressed in a pair of stonewashed jeans, and a trendy little pink silk tank top, Ava wondered if she looked okay. Maybe she should change into something more serious. But then again, who cared what she looked like today? Certainly not Mr. Wonderful.

Charlotte let out an impatient sigh on the other line. "What are you talking about?"

"I have to work this weekend."

"*Again?* You're gonna miss all kinds of stuff. Danni and Rick are getting tickets to Cirque du Soleil."

Ava slipped her feet into a pair of sling back sandals. "Believe me, I'd much rather be hanging out with you…"

"No, you wouldn't. You're a workaholic!"

"I am not," Ava protested, snapping her purse shut.

"About as spontaneous as…as I don't even know what. You're missing out on a room at the best hotel on the Strip."

"Sounds like fun."

"You better believe it'll be fun. Now come on, get that bag packed. If we leave now we'll be there by two."

Ava straightened her white comforter out until it lay wrinkle-free on the bed, and then fluffed the pillows. "I'm serious. I really wish I could, but I can't go this time. I've got to take care of something important. I promise I'll make it up to you, though."

"Yeah, well…I'm holding you to that," Charlotte said bitterly.

The doorbell rang. "Gotta run."

"Call me later."

"Will do." But her infuriated friend had already hung up. Ava sighed.

She opened the front door to find the surreal sight of Justin standing on her step, his hands stuffed in the pockets of his vintage open-weave jeans. Her gaze drifted up to the sage green cotton crewneck T-shirt, then up to the playful expression on his face. The sight of him took her breath away, but she quickly got a grip and realized he was staring at her.

"Is something wrong?" She looked down at herself. Had she spilled juice on her tank top this morning?

His gaze drifted down her body, then back up. "Nope. I've just...never seen you in jeans." He nodded toward her shoulders. "Or...seen your hair down."

She self-consciously fingered a lock. Was he checking her out? Nah. Just her imagination. She cleared her throat. "Yeah, well...come in for a sec...I'm almost ready."

His presence filled the living room when he stepped inside, almost overwhelming her. It had been a long time since she'd had a guy in her house.

She gestured toward the couch. "Have a seat. Can I get you something to drink?"

He shook his head and smiled, but didn't sit down. Instead, he craned his neck to check out her living room and beyond. "No, thanks."

She thumbed back toward the bedroom. "Okay. I'll be...right back."

She grabbed her purse off the bed, and when she headed back out into the living room, he stood scanning her bookshelves. Her cheeks heated up with the realization that he'd probably gotten a good look at her erotic book collection on the middle shelves. Damn. Why hadn't she guy-proofed the house and moved those? *Beyond the Kama Sutra, A Lover's Guide to Infinite Nights of Passion,* and *How to Make Love Until the Sun Comes Up.* Could it be any more embarrassing? If he asked, she'd claim they were birthday gifts.

From the twinkle in his eyes, she knew he'd gotten a good look.

He shoved his hands in the pockets of his jeans and raised up on tiptoes. He cleared this throat. "So. Nice place you've got here."

"Thanks," she replied, tossing her purse strap over her shoulder. She'd scrimped and saved for years to buy the cozy two-bedroom place on the outskirts of Beverly Hills. For the past five years she'd decorated it piece by piece, until it finally felt like home. "Should we get going?"

Outside in the driveway, Justin opened the passenger door and she climbed into his black Jeep Cherokee. She buckled her seatbelt and watched him walk around the other side, discreetly checking him out. *Great arms, great everything.*

He settled into the driver's seat and put on a pair of Ray Bans, protecting his eyes from the already intense Los Angeles morning sun. Unlike her, he seemed perfectly calm about them being alone together, and his "why worry" manner calmed her down a little. He turned the ignition, popped a CD into the player, and then looked over at her. "Where should we go first?"

"I thought we'd hit Rodeo Drive, and then head down to Emery's."

He groaned. "Aw, come on…too stuffy."

"This is research, remember?" she said, folding her arms tightly across her chest.

He buckled his seatbelt. "Yeah, well…I guarantee you…my part of this trip's going to be a lot more fun."

"We'll see about that."

Being in the men's departments again reminded her of the research she'd done to design the beginnings of the Cupid's Beau line. But it was much less embarrassing to wade through an endless supply of garments made to cover male crotches while salesmen looked on when she had a guy with her.

And the research began. "This brand," she said, her fingers stroking the waistband of a pair of red briefs. "Your basic underwear. Comfortable…meant to feel barely there." Ava moved to another rack. "This one…all cotton."

Her fabric lectures didn't seem to upset him. At times she thought he wasn't listening, but then he'd ask her some detailed question and she'd realize that not only was he absorbing it all, he was a quick, sharp study. His non-judgmental attitude and constant teasing smile gave her the impression he enjoyed everything, and she had to admit that being around him entertained her.

Two hours of wading through every pair of underwear she could get her hands on and describing the benefits of the material on every shop on Rodeo Drive exhausted Ava. But she pushed onward, determined to make the most of this chance she'd never have again.

By the time they reached Emery's, she was spent.

Justin turned to her while they stood perusing a rack of boxer briefs, Ava chattering away. "You hungry?"

Upset that he'd interrupted her tirade about the benefits of double-processed cotton, she quit talking and realized she was famished. She admitted his interruption was good timing. "Well…" she stammered. "Actually…yes."

"I know this great Brazilian place on Fairfax. Wanna check it out?"

She shrugged. "Great."

Justin grabbed her hand and raced down the stairs with her in tow, unable to get out of Emery's fast enough. She laughed. "What's the hurry?"

"I'm starving."

By the time they arrived at what looked like a dive, Ava was about to pass out. Inside, with its plain wooden furniture and simple paintings on the walls, the place didn't look like much. Claiming to be an expert on Bosa Nova's cuisine, Justin ordered food for them to share: spinach, pasta, Caesar salad, eggplant Parmesan, two chicken dishes, an assortment of breads, and plantains.

Ava examined the trendy lunchtime crowd and the festive atmos-
phere around them. Two guys came up to Justin. He introduced them to
Ava as two DJ friends who worked at The Study Hall, a nightclub on
Poinsettia in Hollywood.

"Do you know everyone in town?" Ava asked, after they'd left.

"No. Lately I think I just…"

"Get out a lot," she grinned.

He gave her a sheepish smile. "Yeah. Can't be all work, you
know."

When their food arrived, Ava savored a bite of spinach salad and
was instantly sold on the place.

"So how'd you get into the underwear business?" Justin asked, devouring a fork full of chicken curry.

She bit her lower lip and fiddled with her fork. "Uh…"

Justin leaned in closer. "Come on. Was this your life's dream?"

She looked down at the floor and murmured, "Guess I've
just…always liked underwear."

"How'd all this get started?"

She looked around to make sure no one was listening in on their
conversation. Satisfied that no one would overhear, she whispered,
"Underoos."

He laughed. "You're kidding."

"You know…the polyester under…"

"I know what they are, are you kidding? Superman, Bat-
man…which ones did you have?"

"I wanted the Wonder Woman ones," she said dryly. "My mom
wouldn't buy them for me."

He sat back in his chair, his eyes staring into hers. "Who would
deny a little girl with those dimples a pair of Underoos?"

She lowered her gaze. "I decided if she wouldn't buy them for me,
I'd make my own. The woman who took care of our house…she bought

me some fabric and taught me to sew."

His brown eyes widened with interest. "How old were you?"

She shrugged. "Six? Maybe seven."

He stuffed a bite of roll in his mouth and nodded. "Very ambitious of you…"

"Not sure you'd say that if you actually saw my creations." She laughed and dug her fork into the eggplant. "But I got better."

"Apparently." If she didn't know better, she'd think that was admiration on his face when he leaned in closer. "So underwear was always your dream."

"Guess so." She gave him a sheepish smile before taking a sip of banana smoothie.

She supposed his manner worked wonders for his sales career. Make everyone think you were interested in him or her. That's probably how he sailed through life. She, however, didn't know how to do anything but work hard. Despite herself, she laughed at his jokes, and was entertained by his stories. No wonder she'd always seen all of his companions hanging on every word.

"So what about you? Was underwear always in your plans?" she asked.

He took a swig of water. "I don't make plans."

"Then how'd you end up…" She bit her lip, then lowered her eyes. He had a great reputation, and everyone loved him, personally and professionally. How could that have happened without a plan? "Well, you must be doing something right." She fiddled with the stem of her water glass. "How long have you been a consultant?"

"Started my business six years ago."

"And from what I've heard, it's going quite well."

His brown eyes lit up. "And exactly what have you heard?"

Think fast. "I know you have a good reputation. People admire you…"

"Guess so."

Was he blushing? He'd made her reveal an embarrassing detail of her life and now didn't want to tell her anything about himself? He quickly changed the subject before she could point that out.

"You ready for phase two?" he asked, raising one eyebrow.

She took a deep breath, trying to prepare for whatever he had in mind.

Walking into The Pleasure Palace on Santa Monica Boulevard, Justin acted like they were taking a stroll in the corner drugstore. Several racks of erotic cards greeted them at the front of the store. One glance at the glaring full-frontal male nudity and Ava felt all the blood rushing to her face.

Justin grinned at her hesitation and nodded toward the staircase leading to the main section of the store. "We agreed. Research."

With no choice but to go along with him, she sighed. He took her hand, then led her upstairs. A plush, deep red carpet gave beneath her feet as he led her further inside.

"The clothes are in the back," Justin said.

"You've been here before," she whispered, her eyes darting around to make sure she didn't recognize any of the patrons surveying the shop.

"Sure. Haven't you?" He grinned, enjoying her embarrassment. When she didn't reply, his shoulders slumped. "Don't tell me I'm the first guy who's brought you here." He watched for her reaction, and then gently tugged her hand. "Come on."

He led her through several rows of plastic "toys" of every size, and shape. Curious, she stopped to take a peek.

An impish expression on his face, he asked, "See anything you like?"

"No," she said quickly.

Laughter written all over his face, Justin led her to the garment section toward the back. Ava thought she might pass out as they perused the selection. She examined a thong with... rhinestones?

She gulped. "Well...this doesn't leave much to the imagination, does it?"

Justin laughed, unfazed. His matter-of-fact attitude about the world around him was a nice change from her own constant judgment.

She frowned at a black leather thong. "These would look ridiculous."

Justin casually shrugged his broad shoulders, making his way through a rack of boxers. "I'm sure there are people who'd be into it."

"No guy would..."

He gave her a mischievous look. For all she knew he had one on right now. The visual made her blush.

He pulled a pair of red boxer briefs off the hanger and thrust it at her. "Check out this fabric."

She brushed her fingers across it. "It's a polyester/spandex mix." Justin examined at the tag inside, and then studied her, his brow furrowed. "How'd you know that?" She didn't answer, but thumbed through a rack of harmless looking shirts. *Finally. Some normal stuff.* Then she realized they all had racy slogans on them.

He pulled another pair of underwear off a hanger. "How about this one?"

She gave the revealing garment a quick feel. "Nylon and spandex. Maybe fifty-fifty."

Justin read the tag, and then stared at her with a look of awe on his face. "You're good at this."

"It's my job."

His eyes twinkled with triumph. "But...you just admitted...nylon."

"Which leads me to my point. Have a feel and notice that the quality doesn't compare to what we saw on Rodeo today."

Justin gestured toward the racks. "And my point is…the store's nearly sold out of these."

She huffed. "Maybe they don't stock their garment section adequately. They're too busy stocking…" She nodded toward a rack of edible panties. "Other things."

Justin pulled a pair of red edibles off the rack. "Now that you mention it…these look interesting. Maybe we should try these for the Valentine's Day Line."

Ava laughed despite herself. "Fielding would love that."

He took his time checking them out, then decided to check out a rack of condoms with more varieties than Ava knew existed.

Justin had been teasing her all day. Time for him to get a taste of his own medicine. And time to see if he could take it as well as he dished it out.

She perused a rack of sexy men's magazines. When he came to see what she was looking at, she thrust one at him. "Here, I have some reading material for you. Guaranteed to expand your mind."

Justin took a look at the cover. "Might expand something else." He set the magazine back. "But you know, I've never really been into magazines." He leaned in so close she felt his words, and murmured for her ears only, "I prefer the real thing."

A shiver went through her and she felt a strange sensation between her thighs. A warmth flooded her cheeks and she prayed he couldn't see how flushed she'd gotten. *Is it hot in here or is it just me?* Perfect. She'd tried to make him blush and ended up humiliating herself instead. What would it take to embarrass this guy?

"Did you find the condom selection suitable?" she half-whispered.

"Yeah. You might want to check it out yourself. Stock up."

"Great idea," she said, playing along. Then she frowned. *That would be a waste of money, now, wouldn't it?*

Ava shivered in the chilly, still night air while Justin walked her to the front door.

"You cold?" he asked.

She shrugged. "A little." *Or just nervous…or excited about being with you.* She couldn't tell which. After ten hours together, she was sad that their day was over. Sad that today was all she'd ever get. Now he'd go on to other things. On to other women at the top of her coworkers' list.

"I've got a jacket in the car," he suggested.

"Don't bother," she smiled. "But thanks."

They headed toward her front door, where he lingered, scuffing one shoe on the ground. "Think we made any progress today?"

She looked up at him. "Not sure. Do you?"

"Yeah. But…" He took a step toward her.

"What?" she asked. "I'd like to hear any doubts you have. Maybe I have the same…"

He took a few more steps closer. "I think we're being much too scientific about this process."

Too scientific? Was there any such thing? She furrowed her brow. "How's that?"

"Well…you're a woman…"

"Last time I checked," she smiled.

He paused to grin at her joke and moved closer. "All right. Convince me. You're buying a gift for your very charming and sexy lover for Valentine's Day. Out of everything we saw today, which pair of underwear do you choose?"

They'd reached the front door, but she made no move to get her keys out of her purse. "Hmmm…that's tough. We saw a lot of underwear today."

"Yeah…" He moved in even closer, backing her up against the front door. "We saw a lot of things."

Instead of minding the disappearance of both of their personal space, she found herself laughing for the first time in weeks. Months, maybe. "I have no idea. I'm confused. And it doesn't matter, anyway, because I don't have a charming and sexy Valentine's Day lover…"

"Oh, really? No husband, no boyfriend…" He grinned mischievously. "No occasional one night stand?"

She stared up at him and shook her head.

Before she could muster up another thought, Justin leaned down. His mouth grazed her cheek, and she shuddered at the feel of his lips lingering over her sensitive skin.

He paused to look at her. "I've been waiting to do that all day."

She gulped and pressed her back against the wall, glad it was there to support her. "You…have?"

"Your dimples…they're killing me," he murmured.

Unlike that evening in her office, this time Justin gently lifted her chin with his fingers and kissed her. A little moan escaped her at the feel of his mouth, soft and hard at the same time, on hers. She closed her eyes and a rush of sensation took over when he deepened the kiss.

His lips could coax her into anything…he managed to get her to open her mouth for him. A warm rush made her shiver down to her toes when he used his tongue to make her ache in the most intimate places. When he pulled away she opened her eyes and realized his body was pressed up against hers, his arms wrapped around her waist. Through a haze, she tried to get control of herself and figure out where her hands were. She couldn't feel anything. She managed to draw one arm away from his neck, and pulled her hand off…the muscled curve of his butt? She'd been groping his behind?

He pulled away from her. "Should I, uh…go?"

She licked her lips and nodded. "I think that's a good idea." She fumbled in her purse for her house keys.

He gave her one last kiss on the cheek, his mouth lingering over her for a moment, and then headed down the driveway. He turned back and smiled. "Sweet dreams, Ava."

He waited until she got inside the house before driving away, and after he'd gone, she pressed her fingers to her lips. *You have no idea.*

Justin pulled onto Santa Monica Boulevard trying to convince himself it was a good thing Ava hadn't invited him inside tonight. That he'd stopped himself from going further. Given the invitation, he would have devoured her inch by naked inch.

He found her shyness irresistible, and he loved how vulnerable she felt when he'd held her. Somewhere in there, Miss Always-in-Control had a soft side that he longed to explore.

That innocent look on her face, the one that said she had no idea how beautiful she was, had driven him crazy all day. He'd be damned if he didn't want to get her in bed and unravel all her little secrets one by one.

He'd never gotten involved with a woman he worked with. He came in and out of companies, a few months in one place, a few months in another…and never had a problem sticking to his number one rule: no mixing business with sex. He prided himself on the honorable and professional reputation he'd worked so hard to maintain. If he wanted a one-night stand or a one-week or month or whatever it turned out to be, he found it elsewhere. Just too messy otherwise, and he never asked for trouble.

But then he thought about the way she'd kissed him tonight, and decided maybe it was time to make an exception to the rule.

3

Later that week, Ava pinned the last bit of elastic around a pair of boxer briefs on the male mannequin she'd found standing in her office that morning. Leslie, the only person she could think of who'd have the nerve to draw those anatomically correct markings on it with a marker, must have snuck the thing in while Ava was in her morning meeting. Little did Leslie know it was just what she needed.

Ava stood up, brushed her hands together, and paced around the mannequin. She examined the way the boxers fit from every angle. "They look good," she mused. "But how do they feel?" She wished the mannequin would come alive and tell her. No such luck.

She always tested her completed underwear on herself first, and then sewed some mock-ups for Charlotte and Erin. After an initial session in which her friends would tell her if they pinched, bunched, rubbed, or rode up where they shouldn't, she'd have the girls wear their pair all day. If they went to bed with no complaints, the underwear passed the test.

Unfortunately, this time she needed a man. She sighed. That sexy Valentine's Day lover or occasional something-or-other Justin mentioned would come in handy about now.

Frowning, she sat down and drummed her fingers on the top of her desk, determined to come up with a plan.

Ava tentatively knocked on the door to Justin's office.

"Yeah," he called out. "Come in."

She stepped inside and glanced around, trying to be inconspicuous while she checked out the place Justin spent the better part of his days. A glass-top table behind him was stacked high with paperwork and folders, and three white dry-erase boards with colored sales and marketing pie charts hung on the walls. Several cardboard boxes of files sat on the floor, packed with paperwork. The place looked temporary…uninvolved.

Justin lifted his head from an enormous pile of notebooks covering his desk. The second his eyes met hers, Ava couldn't stop their kiss Saturday night from running through her mind. *Don't read anything into it. He probably doesn't think twice about giving every woman he hangs out with a bone-melting goodnight kiss.*

She noticed a poster-size design of the Cupid's Beau logo behind him on the wall. "Is that…for my line?"

Justin watched her. "Yeah, marketing sent that up this morning. You like it?"

She nodded as she sat down.

He placed his arms on the armrests and gave out a relaxed sigh. "So…what's up?"

"I just finished my initial mock-ups for the line."

Justin leaned back in the chair, looking pleased. "That's great."

"Well…" Her heart raced. "I need a model."

He leaned forward and went straight for the keyboard of his open laptop. "Sure, we can order you a mannequin online."

"No, that part's done. I need…" She chewed her lower lip. "A live mannequin. A guy." She watched the mischievous look on his face. *He loves torturing me.* She sighed. "What I'm trying to say is…I need your help."

One eyebrow shot upward. "What can I do?"

"I need you to try on some of my mock-ups. Model them for me and tell me if there are any kinks."

He grinned. "Sounds…kinky."

She rolled her eyes. "By kinks I mean…does the underwear feel uncomfortable…or ride up…that kind of thing."

Justin shrugged. "Works for me."

"Maybe I should…come by your place."

His face brightened. "Great. How about tonight?"

Tonight? Didn't he have a date or something? Besides, tonight wouldn't give her enough time to get used to the idea of seeing Justin Barrett in his underwear. Strictly business, she reminded herself, brushing aside a fantasy about how incredibly sexy he'd look without his clothes on.

"Uh, sure," she muttered. "Tonight's fine."

He grabbed his wallet out of his back pocket, and scribbled his address down on a business card. His eyes met hers when he handed it to her. "Come over after work. I'll make you dinner and we'll do it."

Do *it*? She gulped. "Sure," she managed to squeak out. "See you tonight." She nearly tripped in her heels when she stood up. "Thanks…um, for your help."

She looked up to catch him smiling at her before she slunk out of his office, and then rolled her eyes at herself.

Stopped at a light on the way to Justin's apartment, Ava thought about making a U-turn and heading home. Still, however embarrassing this was going to be, she needed to get it over with and move on. She'd use him for her purposes, and then forget tonight ever happened. She doubted Fielding would appreciate her using Mr. Barrett as her personal human mannequin, but then again, he wouldn't appreciate customer complaints about sub-par fitting skivvies, either.

She parked her car underground in the huge corporate housing structure on Wilshire, the one that made her grateful for her cozy house each time she drove by.

Justin answered the door to his apartment wearing a thin black cotton long-sleeved sweater, a casual pair of linen pants…and she grinned when she caught a glimpse of his apron: "Kiss the Cook".

Don't tempt me, she thought wryly.

Relaxing music played softly in the background, and she smelled something that made her stomach growl. *That's what happens when you skip lunch.* For the third time that week.

She adjusted her sewing bag over her shoulder and cleared her throat. "Is that…barbeque I smell?"

"Yeah." He grinned and gestured inside the apartment. "Come on in."

A plush beige carpet gave beneath her feet when she stepped inside. Nice furniture, she thought, admiring a matching set of comfortable looking couches, and a huge entertainment center gracing the living room. But definitely a bachelor pad. And from the lack of creature comforts and items on the wall, a temporary bachelor pad. *Must be a jetsetter on the go all the time.*

He moved around the place with ease, at home with himself and his surroundings. He nodded toward the sewing bag. "Can I take that?"

"I'll just…put it here." She set it down next to the couch. "We'll need it later."

"Sounds good." He moved toward the kitchen. "Can I get you some water or anything?" he called out.

Come to think of it, she was thirsty. "Sure."

The dining room table set with two place settings made her think he'd gone out of his way tonight. *For me?*

She headed toward the huge picture window in the living room, and checked out the fabulous view. From twenty-five stories up, a beautiful sea of city lights twinkled beneath them.

He came back and stood close beside her at the window.

The feel of his hand on her back when he handed her the water sent shivers up her spine.

"Thanks," she said.

The moment his brown eyes met hers she had no choice but to admit she had a crush on Justin Barrett. A crush that could get her in trouble in every way possible.

"Dinner's ready."

She nodded. "Sounds good." She was so hungry that anything would taste good about now.

She watched him move toward the dining room table. "How long have you lived here?"

He adjusted the silverware around the two plates on the table and set out some napkins. "A few months. Took the place when I got the job before I started with Skiv-Ease." He shrugged. "When this job came along the location still worked."

She stepped up to the dining room table and set her water glass down. She examined the spread before them: steak, chicken, and vegetables all straight from the grill, plus bread and salad on the side. Her mouth watered. "Very impressive."

"Thanks."

Did his cheeks just flush? She cleared her throat. "So…are you…planning on staying in this apartment a while?"

He took off the apron and motioned for her to sit down. "Depends on where the next job is."

"So you…have to move different places all the time?"

"Goes with the territory."

She scooted her chair up to the table. "You just…pick up and go?"

He shrugged. "It's not that bad. The furniture's rented, and I don't have that much stuff of my own. I keep it moveable, you know? Can't collect a lot." He sat down next to her. "If I buy something I get rid of something." Watching her face, he laughed. "Don't worry. It's not that bad." He motioned for her to help herself to the spread before them. "You get used to it."

"I can't imagine," she said.

Ava forked a piece of chicken and some grilled peppers onto her plate. "How'd you learn to cook like this?" she asked, savoring a bite.

"Aw, this is nothing," he said, piling his plate with steak and grilled tomatoes.

"Don't be modest," she smiled. Then her brow furrowed, pressing the issue. "Did someone teach you?"

"My mom didn't cook. And I loved food…so I figured if I wanted to eat I better learn."

She fingered the stem of her water glass. "Well, you taught yourself well."

He chewed. "You don't cook?"

She sipped some water and shook her head. "Too busy working. I'd like to learn one day, though."

He smiled. "I could teach you."

She watched him eat. I bet you could teach me a lot of things, she thought, grinning to herself.

Ava waited for Justin to emerge from the bedroom wearing the first pair of boxers, but wasn't prepared for what she saw when he finally came out. Her eyes widened and she gulped at the sight of his bare chest. Who would have thought he'd have so many muscles underneath the dress shirt? Her eyes roamed from the top of his delectable-looking neck, across to the delineated shoulder muscles, and down to his pecs.

How could a guy eat so much and still have a stomach that flat, she wondered.

She forced herself to unglue her gaze when she flipped to a fresh page on her notepad and scribbled down some comments to distract herself, noticing that her hand shook.

"How do you want me?" he asked, his arms outstretched.

Her mouth watered at the sight of him and she struggled not to think about what those muscles would feel like under her hands. She cleared her throat. "Right there's fine. Um…what's your general reaction? How do they feel?" She pursed her lips and raised her pen in anticipation of his answer, prepared to write a detailed response.

He walked around the living room, nodding. "Wow. They're really soft."

She tried not to focus on his behind. "Does the elastic around the waistband pinch anywhere?"

He shook his head.

She glanced down at her notes. "Good. Can you, uh…sit down for me?"

He sat down in the chair across from her.

"Nothing feels weird when you sit? Do they stretch in the right places?"

He nodded. "They're really comfortable. I can barely feel them."

She pursed her lips, struggling to focus. "Nothing rides up any-where?"

"Nah."

"All right, then. Let's move on."

Ava had nearly gone crazy by the time he'd emerged from the bed-room wearing the fourth pair of underwear, a thong. Her eyes widened. Perhaps she shouldn't have designed them to be so sheer.

"How do those feel?" She feared it came out more a squeak than a question.

"Great." Justin looked up at her. "The only problem is…I feel ri-diculous." He paced across the living room floor, then turned to her again.

"It *is* a thong," she reminded him. She coughed. "A little reveal-ing."

"Not that. I mean, we've been at this for a long time, right?"

"Yeah..."

He stared at her. "And knowing you, we've got a long way to go. I'd be a lot more motivated if you stripped down to your skivvies, too."

She gave him a shocked look, then let out a little laugh. *Yeah, right.*

"Come on," he coaxed. "Cut me a little slack, here."

She stifled another laugh, not budging. Was he serious?

"Come on, I've been standing here practically naked all this time in front of you." He grinned, eyes twinkling. "Vulnerable...exposed."

She bit back a smile. *Yeah, you look reeeeally sorry about that.* She had a hard time coming up with sympathy for him, considering what she'd gone through the past few weeks. Did he think she'd enjoyed blushing from ear to ear since the moment she'd been chosen for the Cupid's Beau line? Didn't he know the mortification she'd endured every time she had to analyze the way a pair of underwear fit some guy's ass?

To top it off, she'd suffered through the evening, wishing he'd cover up that delectable looking chest with a T-shirt so she could quit drooling and focus. "Come on. We've got more to try on."

He got up off the couch, frowning. "I feel so...cheap...used," he muttered, trudging back into the bedroom.

She laughed again. No one would dispute the fact Justin was a fun guy. However, she herself had never claimed to be fun, and no one had ever accused her of it. Maybe it wouldn't kill her to do something a little out of character for once in her life.

Maybe she should do it to prove to herself she could. Just to show that maybe everyone had her all wrong. And shock Justin in the process. Not like he'd never seen a woman in her unmentionables before, but this might throw him for a loop.

She started to remove her shirt, but thought better of it and put it down. What the hell, she thought, shrugging. She pulled it over her head, then slipped out of her shoes and pulled off her jeans. She placed her clothes in a neatly folded pile on the couch and waited for Justin to return.

When he came out dressed in a pair of red briefs with a hint of white striping decorating the seams, she stood before him, stripped down to an ensemble from her very own Conservo line: a pair of unrevealing panties and a crisscross bra.

His eyes widened and he took a step back. His gaze roamed down her body, stopping in various places, and then back up again.

She self-consciously took a step back and stared down at herself. When her wide eyes finally met his, she had a hint of laughter in her voice. "Now you can spread the word around Skiv-Ease that everyone was right." She shrugged. "I warn you, though, no one's going to bat an eye."

He gulped, his gaze glued to her body. "What are you talking about?"

"They sent out a survey about me last year entitled, 'Does She or Doesn't She?'" Ava huffed. "Meaning do I actually wear the underwear I design. Everyone had to check off a box, yes or no."

He gave her an amused look. "And how did that turn out?"

"The votes came in thirty-four to zero in favor of 'She Does'."

"Those are the hottest things I've ever seen," he croaked.

"Yeah, right," she laughed. She'd sewn this particular ensemble for herself and decided to try out a new color. She'd made it an experimental Cayman blue, when customers could order the set in only cream or black. And she'd spent a little extra time creating a soft, curving line through the cup covering her cleavage, just for fun. But still, these were far from sexy.

He scraped one hand through his hair. "Is it hot in here?"

She pursed her lips. "No. But I hope the fact that I'm humiliated now, too, will make you more comfortable."

"Not sure 'comfortable' is the word I'd use…"

"We have more work to do." She knelt down behind him and checked out his butt, trying to keep the process scientific. No choice but to put her hands on his rear and see if fabric wound up in her hands.

"Man, I should be careful what I wish for," he muttered. "What are you doing?"

Still on her knees, she came around the front. "Briefs are the trickiest. I have to make sure there's no extra room…in the rear. Or the front…"

"For crying out loud," he groaned. He rubbed the back of his neck. "What are you trying to do to me?"

"Is there enough room in the…um…" She cleared her throat. "In the crotch?"

"Not with you on your knees in front of me," he said quickly.

"What do you…" Her eyes widened when she got a look at him. She gulped. "You're…"

"Hard? Yeah, well, being around you does that to me," he said dryly. "In case you hadn't noticed."

Was he serious? Were her panties turning him on? She stroked her lower lip with the tip of her tongue. "Not sure I can get a proper assessment of the amount of room… under these…er…conditions…" she murmured.

He dropped to his knees and faced her. "Well, I can think of one way to solve this condition…I mean, I wouldn't want you to get an inaccurate representation or anything…"

"It's very important I get it right," she murmured in agreement.

Justin softly ran one finger down her cheek. "Definitely."

Her heart started pounding. "Do you really like these?" she asked shyly, looking down at her underwear.

"Are you kidding? They leave a lot to the imagination. And right now, mine's running rampant."

She looked up at him and grinned. "So…you have a thing for my underwear?"

He rubbed the pad of his thumb against her dimple. "I have a thing for you." His dark, shining eyes never left hers when he moved closer to her. "That night I kissed you…I thought you might have noticed."

She brought her mouth to his and kissed him. He kissed her back, taking her face in his hands. She let the kiss wash over her and melted against him. He pressed his mouth against hers in an open-mouthed caress, giving her just enough to make her want more. She slid down underneath him on the floor, his muscled chest pressing against her when he settled himself on top of her.

With a little sigh, she nuzzled her face against his neck. He'd be a lot easier to resist if he didn't smell so good, she thought, taking in the scent of him…warm and musky…a total turn-on. She kissed the sculpted edge of his chin, the faintest hint of stubble under her lips.

When his mouth met hers again, one hand caressing the outside of her thigh, she realized he had no intention of stopping, and neither did she.

Ava swallowed the lump in her throat when he planted kisses down her belly. Guess when he said they were going to do it earlier today, he meant it.

She missed the feel of his mouth on her when the kisses stopped and he looked up at her.

She ran her tongue over her lips, searching for something to say, but for once, she was at a loss for words.

He lifted her chin with his thumb and brought her gaze up to his.

The mischievous look in his eyes, the little smile on his face was too much to resist. *Oh, dear.*

His eyes intent on her, he slid one strap of her bra down with his hand, his hand sliding over her shoulder.

She gulped, then slid out from under him and stood up. "Okay, well, if we're going to do this, we'll need some protection." She paced in front of him. "I know you suggested I stock up at the Pleasure Palace...but I didn't think I'd need to..."

He watched her move in front of him, his elbow supporting his weight. "I've got it covered." He laughed. "Pun, uh...intended."

"And, uh, uh..." She frowned. "What else do we need?" She rubbed her chin, trying to think, but it was getting harder and harder for her brain to work. She looked down to find him watching her with an expression somewhere between amusement and confusion in his eyes. He probably thought she was nuts. "We'll need to get prepared, and I think..."

"Ava." He cut her off, laughter in his voice when he stood up. "I'll take care of everything if you go in the bedroom with me."

The impatient look in his eyes told her he wanted her, and for once, she needed to quit analyzing everything to death. No one ever looked at her like that before, and never in her wildest dreams did she think anyone would. She kept babbling, but feeling a little impatient herself, she followed him down the hall.

"Uh, nice, um...paint color," she noted, examining the walls of his apartment. "My mom has a room that's this exact same color, and I really think it's important to get a color that you...that you, um...like...don't you think?"

Without answering her ridiculous question, he reached in the nightstand and tossed a box of condoms on top of it.

Guess I'll shut up now.

In the dark bedroom, she could still make out the writing on the box. "Her Pleasure?" she murmured.

"I aim to please," he replied, grinning. But from the look in his eyes, and the hot, pressing kiss he gave her after he said it, she knew the joking around was over for a while.

In the dim light, she watched the firm muscles of his back when he pulled back the sheets and climbed into the bed. He reached for her, urging her to join him. When she slid in beside him, he put his arms around her protectively and kissed her, then rolled over until she lay beneath him.

He slipped the other strap of her bra down, unhooked it and took it off in record time. His warm mouth pressed against her bare shoulder. The cool air in the room washed over the hot, moist kiss he left there, making her shiver.

"Since we're both almost naked," she noted, staring down at her barely clothed self, "there's no turning back now, right?" Why did she babble incessantly when she got nervous?

He pulled away for a second and looked at her. "You changed your mind?"

She watched him, her chest heaving up and down, and licked her lips. She shook her head. "No." And then she gave him the hottest kiss, one she didn't think she knew how to give anyone, her mouth finding his. His tongue sank into her mouth and she welcomed it, sliding her tongue against his and pulling him closer.

Justin finally drew his mouth away, planting wet kisses over her throat, exploring her down lower, until his mouth closed over one breast. She let out a little moan and leaned her head back, washed in sensation as his tongue kissed, teased and tormented her. He drew one nipple into his mouth and suckled until she ached between her thighs. She was too turned on to resist when he moved to do the same thing to her other breast.

She didn't protest when his warm hand slid inside the granny underwear, his finger teasing, stroking, then slipping inside her, making her wetter.

"Are you nervous?" Justin murmured, his breath warm against her ear, and she shivered.

She shifted her hips. "Yeah, I...haven't...done this for a while."

She felt his muscles tense against her and he made a promise, his mouth against hers. "I'll be gentle."

She grasped the muscles of his back. What were those muscles called? She couldn't think with his hands caressing her everywhere he could reach. All she could do was shudder with pleasure.

"What do you say we lose these?" Justin asked, pulling her panties off before she could answer. She shimmied her hips while he slid them down her legs and tossed them off the bed.

Carried away with the need to feel all of him, she reached down and roughly dragged the briefs off of him.

"Careful. Don't want to rip your mock-up and ruin your life's work," he murmured, his mouth so close, his lips grazed hers. "Not that I'm complaining about…"

"I'll make a new one," she interrupted, her hands stroking the muscles of his behind. She caressed his stomach, and felt his breath draw in when she moved her hand lower, anxious to touch him. But before she got the chance, he pulled away and reached for the box of condoms.

He sheathed himself, and then settled himself against her again.

She felt him enter her just the slightest bit and gasped with the pleasure of it. He moved slowly before sinking in a little further, giving her a chance to absorb every detail of him, to feel the smooth muscles of his shoulders, the feel of his stubble underneath her fingers, the incredible way he felt inside her. Then he sank inside her to the hilt and she thought she may have bit his shoulder to keep from crying out. With a little moan she raised her hips, silently asking him to move, to ease the ache he'd created. He stayed still, driving her crazy with frustration.

"Justin," she moaned softly.

Instead of answering, he leaned down and kissed her. But when his tongue pressed her lips open and sank inside her mouth, it was more than either of them could stand. She writhed against him, and he pulled out, thrusting back into her with a groan.

When he moved inside her again, Ava drew one leg up and across the back of his thigh, drawing him deeper. He moved back and forth, increasing his pace a little each time until she ached with desire, her body craving more and more, reaching for something just out of her reach.

Her open mouth pressed against his neck, and she cried out when she climaxed. She thought she heard Justin groan with pleasure as he moved within her; he fell against her, gradually slowing his movements, until his breathing slowed along with hers.

He rolled onto his side, taking her with him. As if exhausted from his efforts, his eyes hazed over. He leaned in and kissed her.

Her hands caressed his back, noting that a thin sheen of sweat covered his skin. She gave his shoulders a final once-over with hands she couldn't seem to keep to herself. They roamed over the firm muscles, taking enough memory of him with her to last her…as long as she needed. And that could be a very long time.

"Be right back," he murmured.

She watched his gorgeous naked body when he climbed out of the bed. *Did I just have sex with Mr. Barrett?* Her face flushed even more.

This wasn't supposed to be happening. She certainly didn't have road-to-nowhere flings with the office hottie. Or any hottie, for that matter. Neither of her boyfriends had been hot. Nor would she classify the sex as hot. She'd had clean before…and she'd definitely had awkward. Polite…she'd had that, too. But absolutely not hot.

She watched the bathroom door, waiting for Justin to come back. If she could catch her breath she might be able to laugh.

Tonight…definitely hot.

When Justin climbed back into bed, he pulled her into his arms. He kissed her deeply, then pulled away and pressed his forehead against hers. He grinned, brushing a loose, damp strand of hair behind her ear.

"Well," he drawled out, drawing her thigh up over his hip. "You ready for another round?"

Her head fell back against the pillow and all she could do was laugh.

Justin woke up with big plans for Ava and him. First he'd draw her close as he could, then he'd hitch her leg up over his hip, and next he'd run his hands all over that sexy body of hers until they were both ready for a repeat of last night.

He'd thought one night with her would be enough, or at least ease the intense ache in the pit of his stomach…and lower. He was pretty sure he'd dreamed about her last night, and now that he was awake, he wanted her over and over this morning. But he knew he'd have to pull out all the stops in his book of tricks to convince Ms. Workaholic to call in sick and spend the day in bed with him. Maybe he'd bribe her with being her requisite model in exchange for some…favors. One modeling session for every time she…

Her flushed face came to mind, along with her beautiful mouth swollen from his kisses, and he remembered how hot she'd felt in his arms last night. He'd lost himself in her sweet, incredible body, and couldn't wait to touch her again. He rolled over, ready to put his arms around her, but his hand landed flat on the cold sheet. He opened his eyes to find the other side of the bed empty.

"Ava?" he called out. "You here?"

No answer. No water running. No sounds from the kitchen. He hung his head off the side of the bed to discover that her clothes no longer lay strewn on the floor.

He got up and padded around an apartment that had never felt unbearably lonely. Sure did now.

He scratched the back of his head. Ava, a one night stand? Didn't like the sound of it. One night hadn't cut it.

A thousand nights might be a start.

4

Sitting at her desk early the next morning, Ava's attempts to focus on the Cupid's Beau line failed miserably. After an hour, she gave up trying to get any serious work done. Last night had started her creative juices flowing in an entirely new area, and she allowed herself to draw whatever she liked. The result: a sleek pair of black panties with a bra to match. She penciled in the finishing touches and grinned to herself, turning it to take a look from another angle. *Did I draw that?* She shrugged, adding a hint of black lace at the waistband. *Not too bad, if I do say so myself.*

Much sexier than her usual fare, but then again, the most clever, focused woman in the world couldn't design a conservative pair of women's undergarments after last night's ministrations.

She stared out the window with a huge, goofy grin on her face, unable to get Justin out of her mind. His warm hands all over her. Their bodies entangled, his irresistible mouth on hers.

She'd once heard that good looking guys could get away with lying there in bed and let the woman do all the work...not true with Mr. Barrett. From the flush covering his cheeks, the glazed look in his eyes, the exhausted way his body lay beside hers...the effort he'd gone to, to make sure he'd satisfied her, not to mention the patient way he'd held himself back until she'd...she sighed. Not true at all.

She'd managed to fall asleep after he'd made love to her the second time. Too exhausted to hold back her desire, she'd relaxed beneath him while he moved over her, and when she'd climaxed again, she'd clenched her eyes tight, cried out, and wondered if a person could die from pleasure.

After few hours of sleep, she'd woken up to find morning light creeping through the bedroom window. With Justin sound asleep in the bed beside her, she'd gathered up her clothes, dressed, and slunk out of his apartment.

She reminded herself not to read anything into it. Last night was a one-time deal, and the thought made her give out a pathetic little sigh. *I knew what I was getting into right from the start. Besides, I asked to go over there, not the other way around.*

Her mooning came to an abrupt halt when Leslie marched into the office, every blond strand of her short, trendy haircut in place. "Parker, I need to borrow a black charcoal stencil." Her plucked-to-perfection eyebrows shot up to her hairline when she saw the sexy drawing on the desk. "Don't tell me you've giving up your Conservo line." She batted her eyelashes in feign shock. "You don't honestly expect the rich grannies of the world to have to go naked, do you?"

Ava gritted her teeth. "The Conservo line is alive and well."

Leslie crossed her arms over her chest and gave Ava a patronizing look. "Have we given up on Cupid's Beau already?"

In your dreams, Leslie. "Not a chance," Ava replied, casually outlining the hip on the design in front of her. "In fact, it's going great. The mannequin you left in here helped me work out the finishing touches."

Leslie strolled around the office, sticking her nose into everything she could find. With a sniff, she perused Ava's bookshelf next to the desk. "Thought you might need some help. Figured it's been a long time since you've seen a guy naked." Leslie coughed under her breath. "If ever."

Ava forced a smile, and then reached up to make sure her French twist was still in place. "Anything else you need?"

Leslie looked down at the sketch on her desk and frowned. "Those aren't half bad." She held up one manicured nail and examined it. "But I think you should stick to what you do best. After all, not everyone has a talent for...ahem...sexual conservatism."

Ava mustered up half a smile in return for the backhanded compliment. "Thanks for the advice."

A knock on the door made them both turn. Adrenaline coursed through Ava's body at the sight of Justin, and from the way her heart raced, she knew her crush had gotten worse. Did she really think a few hours of rolling around in bed with him would get rid of it?

She knew he couldn't have gotten more than a couple of hours of sleep, and still, his eyes looked brighter than ever, as if announcing to the world he was ready for whatever mischief he could get into that day.

Panic shot through her. Would he act like last night never happened? Big girl or not, could she handle that?

He cleared his throat, stood up straight, and adjusted the jacket of his dark blue Armani suit, a serious expression taking over when he saw Leslie. "Good morning."

Leslie straightened her shoulders, and a seductive look appeared in her cool blue eyes. "Mr. Barrett."

Leave it to Leslie to flirt. Ava knew Miss Party Girl had already gone through enough guys in her twenty-eight years for ten women. Couldn't she leave this one for someone else?

"Just the man I want to see. There are some things I need to go over with you," Leslie purred, slinking up to him. "How about lunch?"

"I'm not available for lunch. But if you'd like to leave your card with my assistant, I can have her set up a time with you when my schedule opens up," Justin replied.

Leslie gave him a sexy smile. "Great." She refused to tear her gaze from him, or move.

A long, awkward pause ensued, and then Justin cleared his throat again. "I have some important business to discuss with Ms. Parker, so if you'll excuse us..."

A confident smile spread across Leslie's face. "I'll just...set up that meeting, then." She strolled off toward the door.

"Wait." Ava stood up and headed for the door, handing her the black stencil she'd requested. "You forgot this."

"Thanks," Leslie said, her eyes glued to Justin when she took it out of Ava's hand.

Justin shut the door behind her, and his shoulders slumped with relief. He turned to Ava. "Thought she'd never leave."

She stared at him, her mouth agape, hoping her delight wasn't too obvious.

Just when she thought she couldn't stand it, her eyes met his. Relief flooded through her; one look in his brown eyes and she knew he remembered every second of their night together.

"You left early this morning."

She ran her tongue over her lips and fiddled with her hands. "Thought I'd...get a move on," she murmured. *And start getting over you.* She fiddled with some paperwork on her desk, covering up the underwear design.

He nodded toward the door, then moved closer to her. "You think Leslie will buy that I came in here on business?"

"Trust me, we're safe."

He backed her up against the wall, cupped her face in one hand, and brushed his thumb over her chin. She shivered. Why did one touch from him make her insides melt?

He grinned. "Oh, yeah? Why's that?"

"The whole company has this list, and everyone knows that I'm at the bottom of it."

He did a double take with a confused look on his face, yet grinned from ear to ear.

She took a quick breath. "The girls put together a list of…they made this list about you. When you first started working here."

He laughed. "How many lists do these people make? What was this one about?"

She looked up at him and gulped before spilling the truth. "Who was most likely to get you in bed. They put everyone in order…"

He looked slightly amused. But not shocked. Maybe everywhere he went women made these kinds of lists. "What does that have to do with…"

"Leslie was first. I was last. The very bottom. As in…no way you'd ever look at me."

He put his arms around her waist and gave her the once-over. "I think we shot that theory to hell last night, don't you? Besides, what do you care about some list they made?"

He had a point. She always let them hurt her feelings, but never stopped to think about why it mattered to her.

"So what…what business did you want to discuss?" she asked, unable to look away from his beautiful mouth.

He leaned in and pressed his forehead to hers. One hand moved up the small of her back, sending shocks of pleasure up her spine so fast she suppressed a shudder.

"Something very important," he replied.

Justin leaned in closer and kissed her. She forgot where she was, her arms moving up around his neck to draw him closer. When she threaded her fingers through his hair, he sank his tongue into her mouth and she gave out a little moan.

The intercom on her phone clicked on, making Ava jump, forcing her back to reality. "Parker. Upstairs. Pronto," Fielding's deep voice boomed.

"Be right up," she called out over Justin's shoulder.

The intercom shut off, but her body still shook.

"You all right?" he asked.

She leaned against Justin for support, her knees about to go out from under her. "He's so loud." *And he scares the hell out of me.*

Justin shrugged. "His bark's worse than his bite." He tucked an escaped lock of hair from her French twist behind her ear. "I should go, though, before I get you in trouble."

You have no idea.

"Have dinner with me tonight," he said.

She bit her lower lip, pondering that one over. "Don't you have a…a date or something?"

He chuckled. "I'm trying like hell to get one. All kinds of things we could do. How about dinner… dancing…" He leaned in so close his lips grazed the shell of her ear. "A repeat of last night?"

A familiar ache coursed between her thighs, her body answering Justin with a resounding "yes" without asking permission from her brain first.

She gulped. "Last night? Which part?"

He buried his face in the crook of her neck, his hand traveling up her blouse. "The part where I…"

Her breath caught in her throat and she grabbed his hand before he slid it over her cleavage. Her cheeks flushed and she grinned. "That one, huh?"

Justin kissed the corner of her mouth before heading for the door. He looked back at her. "We're running out of time here. Do I hear a yes?"

A date with Justin? Was this really a good idea? The last thing she wanted to do was get her hopes up that this could last more than a week. Still, she couldn't wait to see what he had in mind. Just for once, she could take a little chance.

She grinned. "Yes."

Ava sat alone at an outside table at Brighton's Café on Melrose, watching the lunchtime crowd pass her by on the sidewalk. She looked down at her pad and reviewed her notes from last night. If Justin had been honest with her about how the underwear fit, it meant she had few alterations to make, and the Cupid's Beau line was ahead of schedule. Next step: come up with some slogans for the back of the underwear.

"'Be Mine'…" she murmured, then crinkled her nose. "Overused. Hmmm…maybe something like…'Sweets for the Sweet'?" She drummed her fingernails on the table. "Nah… 'Forever Yours'? Don't know about that," she muttered under her breath. "Hmm…how about… 'Marry Me'?" she mused, then giggled, her face flushing. *I think I like that one.* She scribbled it down.

A group of Skiv-Ease employees passed by, including Derek and Leslie, laughing and joking on their way to eat. She supposed the fact that she always worked through lunch precluded anyone from asking her to join them.

The group glanced up at the patrons sitting at the outside tables, but no one noticed her in the crowd. Maybe it was better this way. The new items for her Conservo line had been posted on the Skiv-Ease website that morning, and they'd each have some snarky comment to make about the new slimming line of bloomers she'd created.

She picked at the Caesar salad in front of her. Just once she'd like to fit in instead of always being the odd woman out. Always being the butt of everyone's jokes.

Maybe the success of Cupid's Beau would mean she'd finally be recognized for her work. Fielding spent the morning drilling into her head how important the success of this line was to the company, like she wasn't nervous enough about it already. But at this rate, she might have something special on her hands.

She'd have to come up with an incredible way to get everyone's attention and show them once and for all…and in the meantime, she'd have to work harder than ever.

Ava answered her ringing cell phone.

Charlotte didn't wait for her to say hello. "You're getting your butt to Roscoe's after work tonight. Danni and Rick are meeting us there at seven. And if you tell me you have to work on a Friday night again, I will personally come over there and drag you kicking and screaming out of your office."

Leave it to Charlotte to get right to the point.

"Tonight…I have plans," Ava explained.

"I'm sure you do, but the world can do without a new design for prudish underwear for one night."

Ava tried to think of a graceful way to get out of this. "How about tomorrow night?" she bargained. "Tomorrow night works for me."

"First you turn down Vegas…now you can't come out on a Friday night? If I didn't know better I'd think you were seeing some guy. But since I know that's not the case, I'll expect you to be…"

"I have a date," Ava murmured.

Silence on the other end.

"A date with your laptop doesn't count," Charlotte said. "Now get…"

"Not with my laptop."

"Your DVD player doesn't count, either."

Ava laughed. "Not with my DVD player."

She might have gotten upset with Charlotte's pushiness, but she knew her friend felt personally responsible for making sure she had some sort of social life. If Charlotte didn't force her out every once in a while, she'd never go anywhere.

"I know the date's not with a guy, so why don't you just plan on…"

"It *is*."

"Is *what?*"

"With a guy," Ava whispered, wishing she'd let this call go to voicemail.

A long silence ensued on the other end again.

"You better not be lying about this. If I find out you were in the office all night…"

"I won't be."

"Well." Charlotte cleared her throat. "That's interesting. I presume you're going to behave yourself and wait until at least the *second* date to let him kiss you."

Ava crossed her fingers behind her back. "I will. No kissing. No nothing. I promise I'll be a very good girl."

"I expect to hear all about this supposed *guy* later. Call me tomorrow with the details."

"Of course!" Laughing, Ava shut her phone off.

At eight o'clock, Justin turned around on Ava's doorstep. For a second he thought she'd bailed on him, but she pulled her car up in the driveway a second later, and she rushed out. Her heels clicked on the walkway as she ran up carrying her briefcase, her hair in disarray. He grinned. Very sexy. No lipstick, no make-up…just a healthy flush on her face, and he wanted her all to himself.

He didn't expect anything beyond tonight. He didn't make plans. Only problem was…for once in his life, he *wanted* to make plans. One look at her and he wanted to know he'd get to see her the next night, and the night after that, and get to know every little thing about her.

She gasped for air. "I'm so sorry, I…I got caught up…" She felt the back of her head with her hand, pushing escaped strands of hair back. "Fielding called me into his office because he was concerned I'm falling behind on the designs for my Conservo line's new girdles…I spent an hour convincing him I could handle that *and* Cupid's Beau..." She stopped for a short breath. "I would have called you but I don't have your cell number...and you'd left..."

He glanced at his watch. "You're not even late."

The fact that she was considerate of him and his time...that was something he hadn't had much experience with.

She looked down at herself. "But I'm not ready to go out...and you look..." Her eyes roamed over him. "...all ready."

Justin shrugged and gave her a sly smile. "Maybe we'll have to make other plans."

"How are we doing in there?" Justin called out, rapping on the open bedroom door.

Ava poked her head out from the closet. "I don't know what to wear. Where are we going?" she called out. "That might help."

Justin stood in the doorway.

She looked up and grinned at the delicious sight. "What are you doing?"

"Thought you might need some help."

"Getting dressed?"

"Actually..." He stuffed his hands in his pockets and casually strolled into the room. "Undressed...is more what I had in mind."

She suppressed the urge to laugh, but couldn't stop a little smile from playing across her mouth. "Oh, really?"

Justin pressed up against her body, backing her up until he tumbled her onto the bed. With him on top, Ava giggled and put her arms around him, with the distinct feeling they weren't going anywhere tonight.

"I think the first thing we need to do is take this off," Justin grinned, reaching for the buttons on her blouse. He planted kisses up her throat, then nibbled on her earlobe.

Shivering with delight while he unbuttoned, she rubbed her face against his smooth cheek. "I'm thinking maybe I could wear this new skirt I bought last weekend…"

"First we'll have to take this one off…and experiment," Justin said, reaching underneath her for the zipper. When he got her out of the skirt, his gaze roamed over her and his eyes widened. "What happened to the Conservo panties?"

Through her sheer pantyhose, he looked at the sexy, skimpy black underwear she wore, the design she'd created that morning. She'd whipped up the real thing that afternoon, then tried them on for size in the ladies room. Perfect fit.

"What do you mean?" she asked, trying to conjure up an innocent expression.

"I should have known something was different. You had this look on your face like you were up to some mischief."

"No, I didn't. I never cause mischief," she said, trying her best to sound innocent. "Besides, look who's talking?"

He examined her sexy panties. "So *that's* what you've been hiding under there."

She lowered her eyes. "You like them?"

"I kinda miss the ones from last night. But don't get me wrong…I'm not complaining."

"I don't think I've ever worn stuff like these."

"Then you've never had them taken off of you, either, huh?" he said, his fingers roaming over the lace waistband. His hand slid down between her thighs, cupping her, his fingers caressing her.

She squirmed and lifted her hips while he stripped off her pantyhose, taking the sexy underwear along with them.

She rolled out from underneath and got on top of him, then made quick work of stripping off his clothes and getting him as naked as she was. Deciding she liked the view, she settled herself astride and leaned down to kiss him. She kissed her way down his smooth chest, until his stomach muscles tensed under her mouth.

"You have a perfect tummy," she blurted out.

He took her face in his hands and watched her, amused. "I'm glad you like it."

She leaned over the bed, reaching for her bag.

"Don't go away," he said, one hand on her back.

"Hold on." She pulled out a brand new box of condoms. "I got these after lunch," she announced proudly, opening the box and pulling a chain of small packages out. She grinned and bit her lower lip. "Was I presumptuous thinking I'd be having my way with you tonight?"

Justin laughed, his brown eyes bright. He ripped a package off. "Well, if you're gonna have your way with me," he murmured, his hands sliding over her thighs. "How about we do it just like this?"

She blinked, uncertain.

"Hey, I'll do it however you want," he assured her. "It's just that...I thought you might like it like..."

She reached for the condom and slid it over him. Instead of finishing his sentence, Justin groaned. She positioned herself over him, until he pressed against her wet, slick flesh. Right where she wanted him. His head fell back against the pillow, every muscle in his tight stomach delineated. She leaned down and pressed her lips against his mouth.

"Ava, sweetheart..."

Ava wished she could wait, but she needed to work at this teasing thing. She sank down, her mouth falling open as exquisite sensations flowed through her. Her breath caught in her throat and she shifted her hips, experimenting with how every tiny move she made sent little molecules of pleasure coursing through her.

Justin sat up, his hands roaming over her shoulders, then her back, and kissed her breasts. He lifted his hips beneath her, urging her to move, but she didn't need much encouragement.

They moved together and when she reached the release her body demanded, Justin sat up wrapped his arms around her, climaxing with her. She buried her face in the crook of his neck, feeling his bare, damp skin against hers.

Mine, she thought, when she could finally think again. She leaned her head on his shoulder, her arms wrapped around him. *Just for tonight.*

"I think it works better with you on top." Ava sighed, trying to catch her breath. She leaned against Justin's chest and ran her fingers along the smooth muscles, thinking her grin might be permanent.

"If you'd like some extra practice, we could work on it later," he suggested, climbing out of the bed.

She watched him grab a pile of clothes and head into the bathroom. "You're getting dressed?" she moaned. She reached out for him while he moved away, then collapsed onto the pillow.

"Hold on." He disappeared into the adjoining bathroom.

"Where are you going?" she protested, appalled at the pathetic desperation in her voice. She touched her flushed face, reeling with disappointment. "You're leaving?" she called out.

He came back into the bedroom wearing pants and his button-down shirt. "Think you can get rid of me that easily?"

With a sigh of relief, she rolled onto her stomach, tangling herself up in the sheets. "Then why did you put your clothes back on?"

"To strip them off." A gleam appeared in his eyes. "You like strip shows?"

She laughed, certain her cheeks had turned to their maximum redness. "I dunno."

"Hasn't a guy ever stripped for you?" he asked, buttoning up his shirt.

Still on her stomach, she kicked her legs in the air and crossed them at the ankles, thinking about her completely unimaginative sex life. Stripping had definitely been out of the question. She shook her head, then buried her face in the pillow. "Not even a Chippendales show in college," she giggled.

"Then I better make this good," he announced.

She looked up at him, waiting for the show to begin. A huge, expectant grin came over her face. "No pressure."

She cringed when he perused through her collection of eighties music on the entertainment center in front of the bed. There'd been no time to hide the cheesiest stuff under the bed, but despite her worries, he quickly picked out a CD and popped it into her stereo.

"Oh, yeah. This…this is a good one," he said.

When the music started, he turned his back to her, hands on his hips, ready to start. No doubt in her mind the guy knew how to move. He unbuttoned the shirt one button at the time, then stripped it off. Twirling it on one finger, he tossed it onto the floor. She blushed, and then cracked up. His hand moved down to unbutton his pants. His fingers slowly pushed the zipper down in time to the music.

For the finale, he turned around and dropped his pants, leaving him in only the underwear. By the end, she'd collapsed with laughter on the bed. Something sweet about the show and the effort he'd gone to, to make her laugh, made a warm sensation swell up. And turned her on.

"You're a good dancer," she noted.

"I'll take you dancing sometime."

In the midst of thinking that over, an idea struck.

"Wait. I have an idea," she squealed, her face still flushed. An idea inspired by the sight of him dropping his pants took over. She leaned over the side of the bed and reached inside her briefcase for her notepad and a pen. "Oh, my gosh," she breathed, excited.

He sat down on the bed behind her, breathing hard from his dance efforts. "Damn. I blew it. I was trying to turn you on." He nibbled on her neck, and she squirmed with delight. When she kept writing, he gave out a defeated groan. He reached under the sheet, his hands on her breasts, caressing her. He placed his chin on her shoulder. "What are you writing?"

She leaned back against him, her head lolling back against his shoulders when his thumbs brushed over the hard points of her nipples. "I can't think with you doing that," she moaned.

"That's the whole point," he murmured.

Pleasure flowing through her, she opened the pad. "I just got an idea to present the Cupid's Beau line." Her heart raced while she scribbled away. She turned back to face him. "We can have the guys come in...what if they're...they're doing something, anyway..." She snapped her fingers. "What if they're waiters, but they're really models...and at the opportune moment, they can strip! They can drop their pants, and underneath are all the designs for the Cupid's Beau line!"

He moved around and sat in front of her on the bed.

"And they can have all the different sayings on them!" She bit her lower lip and furrowed her brow, watching his reaction. "Do you think it's silly?"

He shook his head and leaned in to plant a kiss on her cheek. "I think it's great."

Not satisfied with his lips on her cheek only, she brought her mouth to his and kissed him. "Are you sure?" She shivered at the feel of his mouth on her.

He shrugged one broad shoulder. "I'm jealous that I don't excite you as much as a pair of underwear can."

"Are you kidding?" She took his face in her hands and pressed her mouth against his. She pulled away to look at him. "Your strip tease was my inspiration!"

His gaze met hers, his sincere brown eyes twinkling. "Hmmm...speaking of which...I think it's your turn to do a little strip tease."

She gave an embarrassed little laugh. "I need some food first."

"Hmm. Me, too. I'm starving."

"Unlike you, I don't cook. In fact, I burn water. We could order something, though."

"What kind of pizza do you like?"

Her shoulders slumped. "Oh, I…I don't eat pizza," she stammered.

"Who doesn't eat pizza?" he joked. He looked at her and sighed. "I get it. Not into junk food."

Why should she spoil his fun? She brightened. "But you can order it. I'll just have a salad or something." She started to move off the bed. "There might be some coupons in the Sunday paper."

He grabbed her hip, holding her back with one hand. He grabbed the phone with the other. "I'll take care of this."

After he placed the order, she settled herself against his chest with a contented sigh. "Sorry we didn't go out tonight."

"You are? Guess I need to work on my performance…"

She laughed. "That's not what I meant." She gave out a little gasp when he leaned down and pressed his mouth against the pulse point in her throat. "I just mean…I know how much you like going out."

"Yeah? Who'd you hear that from?"

"Everyone knows it. Everyone knows you're the life of the party."

"I'll be the life of our own little party."

She giggled. "Mission accomplished, I think."

"Tomorrow night-"

"That soon?" she laughed.

"I'll take you wherever you want…loud club, Spago, anything…" He cleared his throat. "If I can keep my hands off you long enough, that is."

Later, when the doorbell rang, Justin threw his pants back on. He headed to the door and returned to bed with a large pepperoni pizza and a huge salad. The incredible aroma wafted through the bedroom, making Ava's mouth water.

"Sure you don't want a piece?" Justin asked, eyeing her while he opened the box.

The incredible aroma made her stomach growl. She licked her lips, suddenly desperate to devour some. She looked up at him with a shrug, and then reached into the box. "I guess one piece can't kill me, can it?"

"Thought you didn't eat pizza," Justin said, his eyes wide, staring at the bottom of the empty, greasy box.

She looked at it, too, feeling like a deer caught in headlights. "Who ate all that…did I eat that?" she asked, covering her crammed full mouth.

He gave her a look that said, "afraid so."

She swallowed the final bite of the last piece. "I'm so sorry," she moaned. "I ate all your pizza."

Since when did she pig out on forbidden food? Even if it did turn out to be the best thing she'd ever tasted. Come to think of it, she'd done a lot of things lately she didn't usually do.

Justin gave her a pretend forlorn look, and then picked up the salad container, preparing to take the lid off.

"No, no," she laughed, taking it out of his hands. She set it on the nightstand. "I'll order another pizza, just for you." She put her arms around his neck.

"That won't be necessary." He lowered her down to the bed and planted a kiss on her mouth. "I'll just have to find other ways to be satisfied tonight."

5

"*Marry* me? That's what my ass has on it?" Justin scoffed, standing in Ava's living room wearing a pair of white boxers for her inspection.

Kneeling behind him on the carpet, she ignored his comment and stuck a pin in the fabric. She tugged on the bottom of the boxers, urging him to move. "Turn for me. I need to see them from the front."

He stared down at her, incredulous. "No guy's gonna wear these."

"Relax. Your ass looks perfect." She saw the appalled look on his face and drew her lower lip into her mouth. She frowned. "You really don't like these, do you? I've worked for weeks to come up with good slogans."

He shrugged. "This one's just...unrealistic."

Weeks of slaving away, and he didn't like the one she was most proud of. She sat back on her heels with a frustrated sigh and looked up at him. "Why is it unrealistic?"

"No guy's going to go through all that humiliation."

"What's so humiliating about it?" she replied. "These boxers are fine quality."

"It's not the fabric that's the problem," he replied dryly.

She stood up, thinking this over. "But...what if...what if some guy wants to propose, but he's a little shy and he doesn't know how to do it?"

She paced in front of him. "He won't have to say a word. He can surprise her, and the boxers will do the work."

Justin gave her a look like there was no way any guy would do that.

"Look," she said. "Fielding already made me throw some sleazy ones in. 'Sit On This,' 'Do Me Right'…"

A proud smile came over Justin's face and he folded his arms across his chest. "Actually, I came up with those."

She rolled her eyes. He *would.* "You didn't tell me?" she huffed.

He shrugged. "We went to lunch one day and I just threw them out as a joke. I didn't think he'd make you use them."

"Apparently he liked them so much he's forcing me to include them." She continued on her quest to prove her point. "I figured we might want to have a classy one in there."

He grinned. "Mine aren't classy?"

"'Sit On This'?"

His grin widened, and he didn't look the least bit sorry.

She gave him a frustrated look. How could he not go along with her on this? "Well…they don't have to be only for Valentine's Day. They'd work for just about any occasion. That might help sell more."

When he still didn't look convinced, Ava sat down on the couch and put her head in her hands. She finally looked up to catch Justin watching her.

"You look awfully cute with that pout on your face," he noted.

She grimaced, telling herself not to fall for his act. *Don't think about how gorgeous he looks in those boxers.*

"Look, all I'm saying is…if a guy's gonna buy this kind of underwear, he's probably thinking about getting a piece, not getting married."

She shot him a dirty look. "A *piece*? A piece of what?"

He scratched his head with a sheepish expression. "Never mind."

She frowned at him. "I think we should give them a try." She leaned down and folded a few other pairs of boxers scattered on the couch. "At least…see if anyone wants them." She shrugged. "In any case, I've got a lot of work to do, yet."

He folded his arms across his chest. "You say that like it's my cue to leave."

How could she kick him out? He'd been a good sport. She'd made him come over on a Saturday afternoon and strip for her just because she decided she wanted to try her new skivvies out, and he'd done so without complaint.

She tried to brush past him, but he caught her around the waist and pulled her back against his body. He nuzzled his face in the crook of her neck. She tried to resist, but couldn't stop herself from sagging against him. His warm breath against her neck sent shivers down her back.

"What work do you have left?" he asked.

He nibbled on her earlobe, and she squirmed with delight.

"Talking you into letting me use whatever fabric I want for these," she replied.

He wrapped his arms around her waist even tighter and pressed his mouth against her throat. "What did you have in mind?" he murmured.

"Come downtown with me to the Fashion District? I'll show you just how cheap we could get the fabric I want to use."

He sighed. "Damn."

She turned to face him. "What?"

"I thought you might have something else in mind to try and convince me."

All she could do was laugh.

Downtown in the various fabric shops, Ava bought three bolts of assorted materials. Justin spent the afternoon bored and teasing her while she dragged him from place to place. The guy definitely earned points for patience, she thought, and she had to admit that the whole excursion was much more fun with him.

He came in handy when it was time to pile the bolts into the back of her car, too. Little did she know their shopping adventure would take most of the afternoon. The sun began to set and she glanced at her watch.

"Is it six o'clock already?"

"Time flies," Justin replied, closing the hatch.

"Do you mind if we stop at my parents' place on the way back to the Westside?" she asked, climbing in the driver's side of her car. "They have some photos of my cousin's wedding they want me to pick up. Actually, that my mother demanded I pick up."

Justin settled into the passenger seat and shut the car door. "Sounds great. I've been wanting to talk to your mom."

She raised one eyebrow with a curious smile and turned the key in the ignition. "About what?"

"About why she wouldn't buy you the Wonder Woman Underoos."

Ava checked her mirror and pulled out into traffic. "You are *not* asking her that."

"Come on," he laughed, resting a hand on her thigh. "Why wouldn't she?"

"I don't remember," she replied under her breath.

"You were a bad girl?"

"Probably." She looked over to find him giving her a mischievous look, and couldn't stop the grin that came over her face. "What?"

"I like it when you're a bad girl." His hand, still on her thigh, slid upward.

"Don't distract the driver," she laughed, pushing his hand away.

Ava pulled the car up in front of her parents' house on a tree-lined cul-de-sac in Encino. She parked at the end of the driveway and turned off the engine, prepared to run in and run out as fast as possible. "I'll just be a second."

She saw Justin examine the huge, two-story house and the mani-cured grounds. The one her parents always kept in tip-top shape: lawn raked and mowed, flowers watered, and bushes trimmed to perfection.

"Wow. Did you grow up here?" he asked, straining to get a look at the place.

She nodded.

"Your parents are doing well," he noted.

Ava shrugged. "I guess so."

She looked up toward the house and saw her mother heading down the driveway. "Oh, no," Ava groaned. Had her mother been watching them the whole time?

Justin looked over at her. "What's the matter?"

She undid her seatbelt. "She's already seen you. Now I'll never hear the end of it. She'll assume, by the fact that you're in the car with me, that you're my future husband."

Justin laughed.

"I'm not kidding. And believe me, it won't be funny. She'll ask when we're getting married and harass you..."

"So she figures every guy you're with is your future husband?"

"She sure hopes." Ava groaned. "Neither of us will hear the end of it. I knew this was a bad idea."

"She's in a rush for you to get hitched?"

"You have no idea. If any man so much as comes near me she re-minds me it's high time I settle down. Blah, blah, blah...she drives me nuts."

He touched her arm, calming her panic down a little bit. "It'll be fine," he grinned. "I want to meet your parents. I guarantee I'll be on my best behavior."

She sighed. "It's not you, it's...my mother."

"Come on...how bad can it be?"

She hesitated before opening the car door. "We'll tell her we're business colleagues. And that's it."

He furrowed his brow. "You really think your mother's going to fall for that?"

"Trust me..."

"You sure you want to lie?"

"Well, I..." she stammered, her eyes meeting his. She didn't necessarily want to lie. She wasn't any good at it, but... "I just don't...want to tell her the whole truth."

"It'll be all right. I promise."

No. It. Won't. Grimacing, Ava reluctantly headed toward her mother, Justin by her side, prepared to get this over with as fast as possible.

Rachel Parker raced up to them, looking fabulous as usual, her mass of dark hair piled on top of her head. Did her mother ever wear anything other than perfectly applied make-up and a stylish pair of pants with heels? Even on a Saturday. "Ava! What are you doing here?"

Ava tried to hide the irritation in her voice. "The pictures from Cousin Lou's wedding, remember?"

Her mother gestured toward the front door. "Oh, right. Come on up to the house, both of you."

Ava hesitated. "We can't stay, Mom. We're on our way out..."

"Well, give me a chance to find the pictures." Rachel eyed Justin, giving him the once-over. "And who is this strapping young man? Why didn't you tell me you had a-"

Ava straightened her back and cleared her throat before her mother could get out the words "date" or "boyfriend" or anything along those lines. "Mom, this is my... um... colleague. Justin Barrett."

Justin grinned and extended his hand. "Mrs. Parker."

"Colleagues?" her mother asked, a confused look on her face. She gracefully held out her manicured hand, unable to take her eyes off of him. "What are you two doing out together on a Saturday?"

"We had to go to the Fashion District," Ava said quickly. "For my new line. Mr. Barrett is overseeing the project."

"I see." Rachel finally let go of Justin and led them both to the front door.

Inside the house, she led them into the living room and gestured toward the huge plush couch.

Justin went over to the picture window, which boasted an incredible view of the San Fernando Valley landscape. "Wow. Look at this."

Her mother came over and joined him. "Isn't it wonderful?"

"Yeah. Great view," Justin said, impressed.

"It's not bad."

"And that's a great deck."

"Well, yes…we had that built years ago. There's a Jacuzzi…a barbeque and a wet bar…my husband and I like entertaining out there during the summer."

Justin laughed. "I can see why."

"Can I offer you some tea?" her mother asked.

"We're not staying that long, Mom," Ava said, knowing she would try to get them to stay as long as possible.

Her mother shot Ava a look. "I was asking Mr. Barrett."

Justin walked back to the couch and sat down. He cleared his throat. "No, thanks. But I appreciate the offer."

"Very well." A huge smile on her face, her mother clasped her hands together and sat down across from both of them, crossing her long legs. She turned her attention to Justin. "Well, Mr. Barrett, I'm sure you've figured out by now that my daughter is a workaholic. Does she have you working every weekend?"

Justin grinned and opened his mouth to answer, but before he got the chance, Ava leaned forward. "So, how about those pictures, Mom?" she asked.

"I have no idea where they are."

Yeah, right. Ava huffed, knowing full well her mother had a mind like an elephant and knew exactly where she put them. Why else would she have insisted she pick them up today? "Well, that's why we're here...I've already inconvenienced Mr. Barr—"

Rachel clasped her hands together. "You know, it's getting to be dinner time and I'm alone here...I'm sure you both must be hungry from your afternoon out...why don't you two have dinner with me?"

Ava glanced around the house, hoping her father would magically appear. Somehow she knew better. The house was too quiet. "Where's Dad?"

"In Atlanta for the weekend. He's shooting some second unit footage for the pilot he's working on. So I could use the company tonight."

Great. A guilt trip. "Mom, we um...have to work tonight."

"Oh, work-shmirk. You work too hard. Mr. Barrett, I'm constantly telling her she works too much."

Justin looked over at Ava and smiled. "Me, too."

Great, Ava thought. Both of them together were more than she could handle. "Mom, you said the pictures were..."

"I don't know where I put the pictures right now and I'm too hungry to look. I'll start searching when we come back from dinner."

Sure, after you've tortured Justin and me enough to suit you.

"Dinner sounds great," Justin said. From the grin on his face, he was thoroughly enjoying every second. Ava wished she could relax and enjoy this, but somehow she couldn't bring herself to do it. It was too unpredictable and she had no idea what would come out of her mother's mouth next.

"At last...someone with some patience." Her mother looked at Justin with admiration, then back at Ava with a frown. "My daughter has none. She loves to drop by the house and take off again right away. Never has time for her poor mother."

Please, Ava thought. Would Justin really buy that? It wasn't like her mother didn't have company almost every night of the week. Visitors came in and out of the place constantly, and Ava was surprised there wasn't a party going on tonight.

"Now…how about we go to The Amazon on Ventura. How does that sound?" Her mother smiled at Justin.

The Amazon? Ava thought. *It's such a scene.*

"Good choice. They have amazing steaks," Justin replied. He glanced at Ava with a look that said "this'll be great".

If only he knew.

Ava sighed. Against her mother and Justin she had one choice: to brace herself for a long night.

Just like she knew they would, Justin and Rachel hit it off at dinner. Was there any situation in which Justin didn't feel at home? Any time he wasn't having fun? Ava spent the past hour staring at the jungle décor and listening to him joke and laugh with her mother. Thank goodness someone handled her mother's small talk well. She sure didn't.

"Mrs. Parker, weren't you on that show, *L.A. Vice*?" Justin asked, taking a bite of steak.

"As a matter of fact, I was. How did you know that?"

"The reruns are on every night at eleven. I thought I recognized you."

"Ohhh," her mother laughed.

Did Justin make her mother blush? Ava watched her. She'd never had an issue with compliments before.

"You were fantastic," Justin continued. "My favorite episode is the one where you, uh…had to play a…a…"

"A hooker?" she replied loudly, nonchalant, before biting a piece of steak off her fork.

Ava wanted to crawl under the table and hoped no one was listening to this conversation.

"Yeah," he continued, "to help Detective Russell solve the case…"

"Oh!" Rachel laughed. "That actor…Dennis something or other…he was quite a character. Thank you." She leaned in closer. "I can't believe you saw that! And you remember it so well! Seems like such a long time ago."

Her mother ate up the attention while Ava sat quietly at the table, as usual, feeling invisible. Maybe she shouldn't have refused that glass of wine earlier.

She fiddled with the vegetables on her plate and looked over at Justin. Maybe he liked this kind of scene. Maybe he had more in common with her mother than he did with her.

He glanced over at her and gave her a reassuring smile. She wondered if she had enough to keep this guy interested in her. How long before he'd get bored?

She frowned. She'd have to make the most of whatever time they had.

Later that night, Ava stirred sugar into a latte at a funky little coffee shop on the Westside, shocked that she'd made it through the evening. Most of the patrons had left for the night, leaving Justin and her alone, with the exception of the two baristas.

Ava's knee touched Justin's underneath the tiny table for two they sat at.

"You didn't have to buy my mother and me dinner," she told him. "But thank you."

"Are you kidding? It was my pleasure." His brown eyes lit up. "Hey, your mom's pretty amazing."

She sheepishly met his gaze. "My mother and I have some issues, in case you didn't notice."

He took a swallow of coffee and set the porcelain mug down. "Yeah, I picked up on the tension."

"We just don't see eye to eye. She thinks I should quit working so hard on my underwear lines and spend time working on my personal life. And I guess I'm still mad she used to leave me at home every night with a random babysitter while she went out to party." She sighed and curved her fingers around the small mug. "I guess I should get over it. It was part of her job and came with the territory of being an actress."

Justin's eyes met hers and his hand reached across the table to settle over hers. "You turned out pretty well."

She looked away, her cheeks flushing. Ready for a happier story, she tried to change the subject. She perked up her voice and let her fingers tangle with Justin's. "Enough about my dramas. What are your parents like?"

Justin gave out a deep sigh.

"Come on..." she laughed. "They can't be crazier than mine. Maybe we could stop at their place next."

The corners of Justin's mouth turned down into the first frown she'd seen on his face. She guessed he didn't think her joke was too funny. Maybe his parents weren't together or around anymore and she'd hit a sore subject. Better not to press the issue, but she was dying to know all his secrets. No one could be fun and charming all the time. There was more to him than that...she knew it.

She just hoped she'd be around long enough to find out.

She couldn't deny that she'd enjoyed their time together. He didn't ask too much of her, but at the same time, he acted interested in spending time with her outside of work every chance they got. She wasn't quite sure what the interest was. Though she liked to think he genuinely enjoyed her, she couldn't quite convince herself of that yet.

He watched the baristas putting chairs up on a few of the tables.

"Guess we should go, huh?"

"Yeah."

He grabbed her hand on the way out. Yeah…she'd enjoy this while it lasted. She just didn't know how long that would be.

6

Justin emerged from the kitchen to find his friend Cole Martin kicking his feet up on the coffee table. Cole reached into the bag of potato chips beside him and grabbed a handful. Justin handed him a beer and kept one for himself.

He paced across the floor and took a gulp.

Cole watched him. "What's your problem?" He nodded toward the couch. "Take a load off."

Justin shoved a hand through his hair. "Ah…"

How could he relax? Today was the day. He'd either get the call letting him know his next assignment in Miami came through, or he'd have to start looking for another job tomorrow. On to the next assignment. Another project to devote his time and attention to. Sometimes he wished he didn't have to go through this every couple of months. Every once in a while he wished he had just one steady thing in his life.

Justin jumped when the phone rang.

When he didn't pick it up, Cole nodded toward the ringing phone. "You gonna get that?"

"The machine will get it," Justin replied, raising the bottle to take a swig.

"Mr. Barrett, this is Eddie Denton from TimeSpace Management

in Miami. Following up on our conversation last month...we'd like to have you start the first of September. Give me a call at..."

Justin plopped down on the couch.

"Wasn't that the call you were waiting for?" Cole asked, chomping on a chip.

"Yep."

The moment he'd been stressed about for the past few weeks finally happened: the new assignment had come through. He'd lined up his next gig, so why wasn't he happy? It hit him: he'd be moving on soon, like he always did. One job to the next with no commitments. It never bothered him before. What difference did it make now? One corporate housing structure was as good as the next, so why did the thought of moving to Miami sound so bad? Sunny beaches, great nightlife...he'd always wanted to check the place out, so how had this become a problem?

He remembered his purpose at Skiv-Ease: to assess how to salvage the company and how to reorganize it, or give Fielding the news that they needed to start selling it off piece by piece. Either way, he'd do his job and take off for his next gig. Again. Taking that great reputation and everything else he'd worked for along with him. And nothing else.

"Hey, you're moving to Miami. Where's the celebration?" Cole ribbed him. "What's the deal?"

"Ah..."

Cole reached for another chip. "You love your fast-paced single life. Lucky you can just pick up and go...do whatever you want. Look at me. I do the same thing every day and every night. Gotta work to keep the family going. Don't get married, man. I gotta live vicariously through somebody. Might as well be you." He looked up at Justin, a knowing look in his eyes when he didn't respond. "What are you so nervous for? You got a girl coming over?"

Justin gave him a sheepish look.

"The blonde...what was her name?" Cole snapped his fingers a few times. "The one you met at the bar that night…Alaina?"

"No."

"The one we met at the beach that one time…what the hell was her name?" Cole pointed his finger at Justin. "Katie."

Justin shook his head and reached for the bag of chips. "Ava. I've been seeing her…for a few weeks."

Cole's eyes widened. "Wow. Since when do you date the same girl for more than a few days?"

"You were no better than me, my friend, before Carla."

Cole laughed under his breath and reached for the remote. "Guess she made an honest guy outta me."

"About time somebody did."

Cole kicked his feet up on the coffee table. "Let's watch the game."

Justin leaned back against the couch cushions and folded his arms across his chest.

Okay, so he couldn't deny he had commitment issues. He never lived in a place more than a few months…he could barely commit to a car. He remembered being at the dealership trying to pick out a jeep. When he'd finally found the one he wanted, he'd decided to lease.

But the truth was: he hadn't thought about anyone else since he met Ava. He hadn't wanted to party, unless she was with him. And for the first time, he'd been happy just staying in and hanging out. He'd come to love his new hobby: trying to make her laugh. He couldn't get enough of the way her dimples deepened when she smiled, or her soft mouth, her sexy body. Or the feel of her underneath his hands. Things happened pretty fast and he could feel himself getting closer and closer to something that wouldn't work. How could it when he'd be taking off soon? Too bad he couldn't keep his hands or his mind off her.

The sex was great, but beyond that, he *liked* her. Even when they weren't together, she was always on his mind. Every little thing he learned about her intrigued him more.

But where would this go? How could it work when they wanted different things? He'd move on to his next corporate housing, his next gig. He had to stay mobile. Maybe it was better this way, without her finding out where he'd come from, or anything else about him. One look at her parents' house and he knew they'd grown up on opposite sides of the tracks. How could she not look down on him if she knew?

The closer he got, the harder it would be to let go of her when he pulled his usual pick-up-and-go act. She had a steady job, a steady house…made sense she'd want a steady guy in her life, and he didn't fit the bill.

He'd hurt her before it ended, and if he had any decency, he'd let her go before they got in deeper. Dinner with her mom hadn't been the best idea. Whether he admitted it or not, and even if she hadn't wanted him to meet her, it moved things to the next level. If they kept going on like this, eventually she'd want to meet *his* mom, and he couldn't let that happen.

Cole let out a shout when the game ended. "Lakers lost," he grumbled, turning the empty bag of chips upside down. Justin looked at his friend's empty bottle.

"Want another beer?" Justin asked.

Cole stood. "I gotta go. Promised Carla I'd be home early tonight. And I know you've got a lot going on."

He slapped Justin on the back and headed out.

"Yeah," Justin muttered.

"*I'm* exhausted," Justin said, sitting on his couch.

Ava wrapped her arms around his neck from behind. "Do you want me to cook some dinner?" She planted a kiss on his cheek. "My version of dinner…meaning I get us some takeout?"

"Nah. It's been a long day."

"A long week. Anything I can do to make you feel better?" She placed her hands on his shoulders and gently massaged them.

He got up, pulling away from her touch, and it just about killed him. "Don't think anything's gonna work. Don't have to worry about me."

"You tired?"

"Beat."

She leaned down and murmured in his ear, "How about I bring you dinner in bed?"

"You don't have to wait on me..."

She shrugged. "It's just dinner. Why not?"

Damn. This was going to be harder than he thought. This beautiful woman giving him her attention, and he had to pretend he didn't care. For her own good.

"You know what?" He scratched the back of his neck. "I'm gonna hit the sack. Maybe we should call it a night."

He headed toward the bedroom, and looked back to find Ava nodding.

"Okay," she said, and the confusion and disappointment in her voice registered with him.

Better now than later, he thought. This would only get harder. Better to cut it off now. And he knew when he woke up, it would be over.

"Goodnight."

"Guess I'll...let myself out," she murmured, thumbing toward the front door.

He nodded, forcing himself to let her go.

Justin couldn't leave things like this. He didn't care what happened next...but he couldn't let it end like this. He sabotaged everything that could have any future, that might mean something to him. But not her.

Not this time. Lying in bed, all he could think about was Ava. She probably thought he didn't care about her. How could he let her think that? How could he blow off a woman like her?

He got out of bed and headed into the kitchen to get some water.

A beam of moonlight highlighted Ava on the couch, tousled hair falling around her shoulders. The most beautiful thing he'd ever seen. And she'd stayed the night? After the jerk he'd been?

She slowly opened her eyes and sat up, a startled look on her face.

"It's just me." Justin tried to hide both the shock and the pleasure in his voice at the sight of her. He sat down on the couch beside her, his bare thigh touching hers. "Did I wake you up?"

She rubbed her eyes and drew in a little breath. "I feel asleep?"

It was all he could do not to pull her into his arms.

"Did you stay for..."

"I wanted to leave. I know you wanted me to. Couldn't bring myself to do it," she said softly.

His heart ached. He still couldn't get over the fact that she hadn't run for the hills the second he wasn't Mr. Wonderful. He didn't deserve her kindness or consideration. Or a second chance.

"I was a total jerk. I don't know what got into me...I had a bad day. Took it out on you. It wasn't right."

"Did you want me to go?"

"I wanted you to stay." And he was telling the truth.

She sighed and looked up at him with beautiful green eyes. "No one can be fun twenty-four seven, Justin. You know that, right?" She touched his cheek, her fingers scraping against his stubble.

He let out a wry laugh. "I try my hardest."

She bit her lower lip and smiled at him. "Yeah. I noticed."

One look at her eased the hollow ache inside him. "I'm glad you're here." And he meant it. He took her face in his hands. "I'm gonna take you to the best breakfast you've ever had in the morning. How about that?

Spend the day together?"

She nodded. The feel of her hands on his face…Justin couldn't stand another second. He leaned in and kissed her, her lips soft and sweet against his. Her mouth opened, welcoming his tongue.

He pulled away, letting his eyes meet hers. "You forgive me for being a total jerk?"

She nodded, pressing her forehead against his. "I thought you didn't want me anymore."

"Because of the way I acted?"

"Yeah."

He brought his face down to hers and kissed her again. "I'm sorry."

When he kissed her again, he felt her sag against him, and gently lowered her onto the couch. She let out a little moan and reached for him, but he pulled away while he still could.

"Don't go anywhere," he murmured, getting up to go get some condoms.

Ah, hell, he thought.

When he joined her again on the couch, he tried to forget that he'd be off to Miami when he finished here. All he could think about was the incredible way she felt under his hands, her soft skin, and that look on her face he couldn't resist.

One hand slid down the flat of her warm stomach and between her thighs, and with a whimper, she opened them for him. His fingers pressed into her soft flesh, teasing and exciting her. He moved lower, kissing the soft flesh of her inner thighs.

The flush on her face deepened and her breath came in soft pants. He moved between her thighs, against her slick flesh. He rested there for a few moments before he sank into her.

"Oh, Justin," she moaned softly. "I can't wait…"

When her hips raised up to meet his, it was more than he could stand. He moved as slowly as he could at first, until he heard her groan again beneath him, asking him for more. He increased his pace until his fast moments gave them both an intense orgasm.

Ava cried out, and he thrust deeply as he gave in to his own climax. She moved her hips against his, drawing out the last waves of pleasure. When it was over, soft moans escaped her. He withdrew from her slowly.

When she wrapped her arms around him, her hands stroked up and down the length of his back, her breathing deep and ragged. She sighed sleepily. "That was…um…"

"Yeah," he murmured, feeling totally content for the first time in a very long time. How would he leave her? He couldn't think about it tonight.

"Come to bed with me," he said.

She crawled into the bed with him and she lay there, entwined with him. Neither said anything. His hands roamed over her body, the curve of her hips, and then the perfect shell of her ear. She curled her fingers against his chest.

She gave out a soft moan and settled her body close up against his. His only thought as he drifted off was that maybe she hadn't been as off track with the "Marry Me" boxers as he'd thought.

7

At two a.m. a few days later, Ava lay wide-awake in bed. A set of shiny
rhinestones across the front of one of her thongs refused to lay flat enough
and had driven her crazy that afternoon. Now she'd dreamed about how it
didn't look right. Nightmares of everyone taking one look at it and laughing, pointing and cringing at the upcoming gala made her bolt awake.

Justin lay beside her, sound asleep. He'd come over at midnight,
after an executive briefing that went late into the evening, exhausted. He
promised to buy her breakfast at Mimi's Café in the morning if she'd save
him from driving all the way home and let him crash at her place that
night. She hoped that was just an excuse to see her.

She tiptoed out of bed and piled her hair on top of her head in a
bun, securing it with a few bobby pins. She slipped on a light silk robe
that matched her skimpy nightgown, one of her own recent creations, and
headed into her office to get some work done.

After removing the offending rhinestones on the thong, she gathered up some smaller ones in her sewing kit to experiment with. She
found the right sized needle and threaded it, and then sewed the little
rhinestones on by hand, one by one.

"Hey."

She turned toward the deep voice to find Justin standing in the doorway in a pair of boxer briefs, arms folded across his chest. Beams of light from the hallway accentuated his gorgeous, smooth skin. She grinned.

"Caught you." He came up behind her and wrapped his arms around her neck. She jumped and squirmed with delight. He placed a kiss on the back of her neck, the place he always touched to make her tingle all over. "Coming back to bed?"

"Soon." As anxious as she was to get her work finished, she loved the distraction.

He nibbled her neck while placing tiny kisses on her sensitive flesh, and she bit back a moan. She indulged in a shiver that ran through her, turned her head, and noticed the time. "Is it really after two?"

"Yeah."

"Time flies when you're having…" She gave out a little squeal when he wouldn't quit kissing her. She smiled from ear to ear, certain that whatever he had in mind would be a lot more fun than what she was doing.

He placed another moist kiss on her neck. "Thought you might need some extra inspiration. I'll strip if you want."

She looked down at his boxer briefs and teased, "Are you that easy?"

"For you…yeah."

She held up the thong. "I might take you up on that later." She turned around in the chair and started the finishing touches.

He headed back toward the doorway and lingered there for a few minutes while she worked. He finally cleared his throat. "So. How much longer are you going to work?"

"Just a few more minutes."

He shot her a doubtful look. "How about I read you a bedtime story?"

She furrowed her brow as he mysteriously disappeared out of the office before she answered.

Curious about what he was plotting, but pretty sure he had something naughty in mind, she finished her rhinestone work, turned out the office light, and headed back to the bedroom. She dropped her robe on the floor and slid under the covers.

When he didn't appear in a minute, she called out, "Justin? Where are you?"

He propped himself against the doorframe of the bedroom, opened a huge book, and began reading.

"What's that?" she asked, craning her neck to catch the title.

He tilted the cover so she could read it: *Beyond the Kama Sutra.*

"You've got to be kidding." She laughed and sat back in the bed, folding her arms across her chest. "That's not a bedtime story."

"Sure, it is. This is great stuff." He came into the room and placed it in her lap. "Go on, read it."

She laughed. "I will do no such thing."

"Come on," he urged.

"I can't read this…"

"It's your book."

"Where did you find this?"

"On your shelf." He moved to the other side of the bed and crawled in beside her. "Actually, I saw it the day I came over and we went on our little field trip. And since then I've been wondering…if you'd like to try any of this stuff out."

She quickly shook her head.

"Come on. It'll be fun." He turned a few pages and pointed to one particularly lurid drawing of two entwined bodies. "How about we give this one a try?"

She blushed three hundred shades of pink. "I don't think so."

"This one doesn't do it for you? Okay, then pick out your favorite one," he teased, grinning at her. "We'll give the one you've always wanted to try a shot."

She giggled, about to die of embarrassment.

"Either pick your favorite, or I'll make you go through and mark all the ones you've already done."

"Ha! That wouldn't take long," she said. She laughed and bit her lower lip. He looked at her with an expectant look on his face. Might as well play along. Maybe she could find something that would shock him. *As if that's possible.*

She blushed even deeper and pointed to a picture of a couple in a position she didn't think two people could get in. "This one."

He raised one eyebrow, as if surprised at her choice. "Really?"

She looked up at him through her lashes. "You think it's possible?"

"Sure," he said, totally unfazed. He placed his hands behind his head, fingers entwined. "People have been doing that one for thousands of years."

"Oh, really?"

She didn't know why she had so many doubts. Knowing him, he'd find a way to make it work.

"Let's keep up the tradition," he grinned.

"I thought you were exhausted."

"Not *that* exhausted."

Ava laughed as he reached for her and took her in his arms.

Friday morning, Ava headed into the break room at Skiv-Ease to grab a can of juice out of the fridge, but familiar voices stopped her just outside the door.

"I can't believe they haven't taken the line away from her yet," she heard Derek say.

Someone popped a soda can open.

"Probably too late to start over," Leslie replied. "They probably have to go with whatever she designed. Maybe they had to change it to the 'Grumpy Grandpa' line. She can design for both granny *and* grandpa now."

Derek burst out laughing.

"I don't get it," Leslie said, in between what sounded like sips of a drink. "There's no way in hell she's pulling this off."

"Unless she has a secret life," Derek replied.

"What life?" Leslie laughed. "She's always here working."

"It's possible…"

"Please. She's so uptight she's probably never even kissed a guy."

Ava frowned. A long pause ensued, and just before she decided to step into the kitchen and join them, Leslie continued.

"I did see her drawing this sexy pair of underwear the other day, though."

"You sure she drew it?"

"I saw her marking on it!" Leslie's voice rose an octave. "It was on the desk right in front of her. She had to have."

"No way." Derek's tone suggested that Leslie had lost her mind.

Leslie huffed. "I can't take this anymore. I'm gonna sneak into Little Miss Innocent's office and see what she's come up with."

Someone popped another can open.

"Good luck. She's probably locked them up," Derek said.

"I don't care," Leslie replied. "I'll find a way."

"You'd better keep your mouth shut about them. Those designs are supposed to be a secret until the gala dinner."

Leslie's voice started at one side and ended at the other side of the room as she paced across it. "This is crazy! Miss Prude must be doing something right, and I want to know what the deal is."

Ava held her head up high and adjusted her conservative black jacket. She'd always known what everyone in the company thought of her, but she wished they'd be more careful to keep it to themselves.

Did Justin think she was a prude, too? He always assumed she'd done a lot of stuff she hadn't. Then she'd break the news to him that it was new to her. Maybe he thought she'd lived the life of a nun, and when he teased her it was only in fun. He always acted like they had a good time together. She'd loosened up a lot, that was for sure.

She'd even indulged in his "bedtime story" last night.

Suddenly not as thirsty as she'd thought, she turned on her heel, deciding to conduct an experiment. See if she was really as prudish as everyone thought.

"When are you going to bring home a nice young lady?" Jennifer Barrett asked, putting a glass of lemonade on the kitchen counter in front of Justin.

"Come on, Ma," Justin groaned, grabbing the glass.

He rolled his eyes and took a gulp. Why did they have to go through this every time he came to visit? He sat at the kitchen table, taking a load off. Exhausted and thirsty from a Saturday mowing her lawn in the middle of a warm afternoon, he wished she'd let him turn on the AC. Since she refused, on the grounds it cost too much money even when he insisted on paying the bill, he'd have to rely on lemonade to cool him off.

He'd kill for a shower about now, or at least a clean shirt to replace the soaked one he had on, but both would have to wait.

"Didn't you have that neighborhood kid mowing the lawn?" he asked, finishing off the glass.

"He still does," his mother replied, sticking her head into the refrigerator. "When he bothers to show up."

Justin slumped in the chair and looked outside the kitchen window, inspecting his mowing work. At least the lawn looked pretty good. "Took a lot of time to mow this time. The grass was long."

"You *do* like girls, don't you?" she asked, removing some lunchmeat and mustard to make sandwiches. "You never bring anyone home. I'm beginning to think you're not interested."

Justin rolled his eyes again.

"You should go out and have some fun."

She tousled his hair.

"Now, you just have to remember to be safe…"

Justin jumped up from the chair cleared his throat.

"So, Ma, how about I take you to the hardware store next weekend?"

"What for?"

"To fix the place up, remember? You can pick out some paint you like and we'll start with the kitchen." Justin glanced around. "For starters I'll get rid of these old wood panels… paint the walls a nice color."

His mom pursed her lips and starting putting a sandwich together. "The kitchen's fine. Besides, I'd rather spend my money buying yarn for my knitting. Not on paint."

Justin scrubbed his brow with the back of his hand. "I've got plenty of money to fix this place up *and* buy your yarn, too, Ma."

His mother frowned. "I should be buying you things," she muttered, starting to make a second sandwich.

"Don't make me food. I have to leave."

"You can take it to go."

Justin knew better than to argue.

"We've been over this before," his mother continued. "You've done enough for me. Don't you dare spend your money on me." She looked around her tiny, rundown bungalow. "Besides, I like it just the way it is. Unlike you, I don't like change. There's nothing wrong with this place. And if it ain't broke, don't fix it."

"We could forget the home improvement if you let me move you to a nicer house."

"How many times do I have to tell my son I don't want him spending his hard-earned money on me? Especially…moving me." A scowl came over her face. "Ridiculous."

"I don't like you being in this neighborhood."

She stubbornly pursed her lips. "I raised you here. I'm not moving."

"I might be moving to Miami and I want to know you'll be in a safe place."

"Don't tell me you're moving away *again*," she said, panic in her voice. "When did this come up? When you moved back from New York last year I thought it was for good."

Justin shrugged. "Gotta go where the jobs are."

"You're all I've got, you know."

"I'm never anywhere long." He stood up and washed the glass in the sink. "After Miami who knows where I'll end up. I could be back here."

"All my friends are here. Where would I go, Justin?"

Justin let out a grunt of frustration. "Sherman Oaks? Burbank? I know you like your poker nights, but..."

"It's not just that. We watch out for each other around here. Nothing's going to happen." Libby, her golden retriever, ran into the kitchen and ran up to Justin, wagging her tail.

"Besides, I can have my dog here."

His mother smiled at her Libby.

"I swear, sometimes I think she likes you better than me."

Justin gave Libby a few pets. "We'll find you two a place with a big yard."

She carefully laid lunchmeat into the sandwiches and spread some mustard on the bread. "It'll be expensive."

Justin rolled his eyes. "Would you let me worry about that? I told you, it's not a problem."

"I know how hard you work." She wrapped up a sandwich in foil and thrust it toward him. "Now get out of here. Unless you want to put up some money for the game tonight."

He took the sandwich, knowing better than to refuse it. "Nah, I gotta get going."

"You'll be back tomorrow?"

"Yeah, I'll finish trimming the lawn."

"I'm sure you have things to do tonight."

"I'll see you tomorrow. Love you." He planted a kiss on her cheek and headed for the front door.

"Go out tonight and find yourself a nice young lady!" his mother called after him.

Justin shook his head and smiled despite himself. Did his mother ever give up? He grabbed his keys out of his pocket and got in the car. If only he could show off the "nice young lady" he'd somehow managed to find. Ava was definitely the kind of woman he could bring home to mom, but…what would Ava think when she saw where he'd grown up? His mother didn't take care of herself, and she couldn't care less about wearing nice clothes or keeping the house fixed up.

He drove out of the run-down neighborhood deep in the Valley, thinking it couldn't be further away from where Ava had grown up. He was always the poorest kid, even in the dumpy schools he'd gone to. He'd gotten laughed at so much in middle school for his second-hand clothes, harassed because he never had money to go on fieldtrips, and tortured because he never had lunch money. Most of the time he went without.

His mother worked her ass off waiting tables to make enough money to make ends meet, but it was never enough. Still, he'd never forgotten that she'd done the best she could for both of them.

Tired of the harassment, and wanting more, he decided he wanted things to be different after middle school. He got enrolled in a high school further away where nobody knew anything about him, and reinvented himself. He opted to become charming and fun, and they'd be too busy laughing with him to realize how poor he was. The plan worked.

Smiling at the sandwich his mother made, he unwrapped it and took a bite.

He loved his mom, always had, and admired her for raising him the way she did, with no help from anyone and no money, but he wanted her to do more for herself. He never gave up trying to give her money to buy clothes, to go on a trip, to buy a new car, but she was too proud to take much of it. She seemed content with her modest lifestyle, maybe because it was all she'd ever known.

What would Ava think of him if she knew about his past? And her mother? Would Rachel Parker want her only daughter dating someone like him? A guy who'd never met his father because he'd disappeared six months before Justin was born? A poor guy whose mother raised him alone on a series of waitressing jobs?

What would he do if Ava wanted to see where he'd grown up? Nah. He couldn't ever let her do that. That would be the end of it.

When Justin got home, he couldn't wait to see his "nice young lady." He showered, dressed, and drove straight to her place, but her car wasn't anywhere in sight. Then he remembered she was working at the Beverly Hilton that afternoon. He decided to head over to the gala room and surprise her. He'd take her somewhere impressive for dinner tonight and ease the stress after the hard day she probably had.

In the huge gala room at the Beverly Hilton, Justin watched her with admiration while she examined the male models strutting around the room. They each wore a pair of her skivvies. His smile faded as he glanced at them. Where did they find these guys? Jealousy coursed through him.

Meanwhile, Ava focused entirely on the task at hand: her creations and her work. Jealous or not, he'd never been so proud of anyone. He'd never seen anyone work so hard on anything in his life. He admired her, the way she wouldn't give up on something until she got it right. It wasn't his style…since high school, he'd skated along on his charm, swindling and weaseling his way into whatever he needed with minimal effort. If one thing didn't work, he moved on to something that would.

A model dressed in a thong covered with rhinestones stroked Ava's arm for attention. Justin scowled, feeling a pang of jealousy go through him.

Ava looked at the other guy's asses, adjusting their underwear. He knew this was just her job, but what he wanted was for her to check *his* ass out. He couldn't wait to get her alone and all to himself, and it was all he could do not to grab her and take her away right now.

He casually walked past, and her eyes sparked at the sight of him. She looked shocked. Damn. He couldn't exactly take her in his arms in front of all these people.

He nodded, pretending to supervise her work. "Ms. Parker."

She nodded back. "Mr. Barrett."

He nodded toward one of the corridors off the main room, then headed in that direction.

She joined him a minute later. "What are you doing here?" she giggled, as if having the time of her life. "Why didn't you tell me you'd be stopping by?"

"Thought I'd surprise you," he said with a grin.

Her brow furrowed when she saw the look on his face. "What's wrong?"

She turned around to make sure no one was looking, then took him in her arms. Relief came over him as her softness pressed against him.

He nodded toward the commotion down the hall. "So what's with those guys out there?"

"What?" she laughed.

"Mr. Rhinestone thong. What's the deal with him?"

She shrugged. "Not a clue."

"The guy seemed kinda touchy-feely."

"He's harmless."

"Yeah, well, he seemed to be enjoying you checking out his ass," he grumbled.

Her green eyes lit up. "Yeah? I'd rather check yours out," she said with a mischievous grin, and he felt her hand grab him from behind.

That's it. He pulled her up against him and ground his mouth against hers.

While she sat facing him in his lap on her bed, Justin successfully got Ava naked… except, he gulped, for the…undergarments she had on. *If this can be called an undergarment.*

"Ava, what's with this…"

She put one hand on the thin line of rhinestones, the only thing preventing the thing from slipping off. "You don't like these?"

He groaned hungrily and stroked his hand against her soft hip. "Oh, I like 'em…it's just…uh…where'd you get them?"

She chewed on her lower lip. "I made them. What's the matter?"

He shrugged. "Not your usual style, that's all."

She looked into his eyes. "Do you think I'm a prude?"

He chuckled. "What?"

"Do you?"

He paused, then gave her a huge grin, his brown eyes sparkling. "Yeah. I get off on it, though."

She climbed off him, clearly about to get out of the bed.

He grabbed her thigh, not letting her get away. "Hey, what's wrong? I'm just kidding."

She pouted and glared back at him. "You do think I'm a prude."

"Whoa. Where'd this come from?"

"Everyone at work thinks I am."

He groaned and lay down beside her. "Work people again? What do you care what they think?"

She shrugged, but looked at him like she very much cared what they thought. He wondered why she let them get to her. But he understood. He'd been through this. Spent his whole life caring what people thought.

"Did you ever think that they're jealous of you?"

"Jealous? But why would they…"

He planted a kiss on her hip. "Why wouldn't they be? You're classy…talented…gorgeous…"

Ava blushed. "But they're always teasing me…making fun of my work."

He settled beside her, spooning up against her back. "You don't have to prove anything to me or to them."

She turned and ran her fingers over his chest, then leaned her head against him. "Do you ever think I'm…not that great in bed?"

He raised one eyebrow. "When have I ever said that?"

"You didn't, I just…thought you might think that."

"What did I do to make you think that?"

"You didn't…" She broke off, and that's the only explanation he got.

"Sweetheart, I wanted you the second I saw you," he said finally, when the silence got to be too much.

"But you thought I was a prude."

"What's with the prude thing tonight? I thought you were hot. What else do you want me to say?"

She pondered that for a minute. "You really thought I was hot?"

"You want the truth?"

"Yes."

He gave out another deep sigh, his fingers sneaking under the thong she wore. "All right. Fine. My first thought? I wanted to get you out of that suit and into bed as fast as I could."

"But you didn't think I'd do it?"

"I didn't know. I was hoping, though. What's the problem? I liked it that you seemed so shy. Part of the package. And I like the package…" He nibbled on the soft skin of her shoulder.

"You thought I'd be able to resist you?"

He stroked one hand over her back. "I was hoping if you did, I could wear you down." He tried to pull the thong down, running his hands along the inside. "This thing…it's sexy, sweetheart. But it can't be comfortable."

She laughed. "Not at all. It needs a lot of…"

He covered her mouth with his before she could finish.

He wondered how she could be so insecure with herself, with her beautiful little body and her talented mind. She had it all. He was the one who had something to hide, the one who kept secrets. He pushed the worry away. He didn't want to think about his, not with her in his arms. He just wanted to enjoy their time together.

Face it. I'm falling for her.

And there was nothing he could do to stop it.

8

"*Could* you look any hotter?"

Ava examined the bewildered expression on Charlotte's face while they stood in the dressing room of Romina's Boutique on the Third Street Promenade.

Smoothing down the skirt of the very sexy black dress she'd picked out for the gala she asked, "You like it?"

"Are you kidding me?" Charlotte's eyebrows shot up. "You're going to cause some heart attacks at this thing."

Laughing, Ava replied, "Yeah, right." She turned her hip and glanced in the mirror to check the view from the side. She frowned. "Still...I guess it's not bad."

"Not bad? You *have* to buy this one. It fits like it was made for you."

Testing to see what she'd look like, she put her hair up with her hands and took a look in the mirror. She sighed, and then gave the dress her nod of approval. "I think you're right."

So what if it cost a little more than she was usually willing to pay? It fit perfectly, and she wanted to look good.

Charlotte held the door her as they headed out. "So this event is a big deal, right?"

Ava nodded, a garment bag containing the dress over her arm. "Oh, yeah. Very. Hey, let's go get you that strapless bra you need for your bridesmaid dress."

Charlotte screwed up her face. "It can wait."

Ava got a better grip on the garment bag. "No, it can't. The wedding's in a few weeks." She urged her friend along. "Come on, there are some nice shops here."

Charlotte kept her feet planted firmly on the sidewalk. "It's okay."

"What's the problem?"

"You know we don't have the same taste," Charlotte said. "I don't go for the geriatric look." She waggled her eyebrows, a huge grin on her face.

"Afraid I'll ruin your chances with some hot groomsman?"

"Damn straight," Charlotte laughed.

Ava frowned. *Am I that bad?* She stopped to peer in the window of Paris Panties, a boutique with upscale underwear and casual clothes. She cleared her throat. "Believe it or not, I may have designed my last conservative undergarment."

Charlotte let out another laugh. "Yeah, right."

"I'm not kidding!"

"You have to be. Everyone knows it's your life. Why are you thinking about changing your style?"

Ava looked inside the shop. "I don't know, I just...I didn't think I'd have this much fun designing sexy stuff." Deciding the place had potential, she headed toward the front door. "Let's go in. We might find you something in here."

"But you love granny wear! That's what I love about you!" Charlotte said, traipsing inside behind her. "It's part of your charm." She headed toward a small rack of adorable nightgowns. "Does this have anything to do with that guy you're seeing?"

Shrugging, Ava shot her a secretive smile.

Charlotte gave her a skeptical look before thumbing through the gowns. "You guys aren't…you know…" She looked around to make sure no one was listening, then whispered, "Doing it?"

Ava batted her eyes with feigned shock at Charlotte's suggestion. "Of course not. He's never laid a hand on me."

Charlotte's eyes narrowed. "You little liar," she teased. "Well, no wonder you're spicing it up…most guys don't want to undress their woman only to discover some hideous undergarment. Kind of a turn-off."

Ava thumbed through the other side of the rack with a sly grin on her face. "Actually, he likes my Conservo line." She found a rack of sexy bras and started looking through them.

"So why change your style?"

"Well…I like the sexier stuff. I never thought I'd get into it." She held up a black strapless with a soft, very feminine line along the bust. "Speaking of which, how about this one?"

Charlotte shrugged and smiled. "You're the expert."

Justin watched Ava through the conference room glass, sitting across the table from two women with the events planning committee. She'd been worried about this meeting for days, wanting every detail to be perfect on gala night. She looked so serious and professional… determined. He watched her delectable mouth while she spoke, and her sexy little dimples when she smiled.

Perseverance had never been a turn-on for him, but he'd be damned if Ava's didn't make him sit up and take notice. He wished he could be that enthusiastic about his work, but whether he was good at it or not, it never gave him any real satisfaction.

He watched Ava nodding at something the women said. Unlike the first time he'd seen her, she held her head up high, a new confidence evident. Like deep down she knew she'd pull this off. And that excited flush on her cheeks was something he'd never seen before. Except maybe after he'd given her multiple orgasms last weekend and she lay breathless and exhausted beside him. The thought gave him a satisfied grin.

Life had changed the last few weeks. Half the time he couldn't concentrate on anything but figuring out how to get her naked again. Maybe breaking out that Kama Sutra book wasn't the best idea. Now instead of his mind being on work, all he thought about was going through it and doing every single one of those positions again, page by page.

Nah, he thought, laughing to himself. He wouldn't take back insisting they try the stuff in that book. They'd had too much fun with it.

A group of four employees approached, on their way to a meeting. Justin pretended to look for something in one of the file cabinets so no one would catch him staring at Ava.

"Hey Justin, how about drinks after work?" Mark Peterson asked. "A couple of us are heading to Rodney's for martinis."

"Yeah, I might do that," he said, noting that all four stared at him. He did a double take. What did those knowing smiles mean?

Mark stuffed his hands in his pockets. "See you tonight."

Justin scratched his head. "Uh…sure."

"We owe you a beer, man," Mark said under his breath. He gave Justin a rough pat on the shoulder before the group disappeared down the hallway.

He took a guess at what the happy looks meant. Rumors spread like wildfire through the company. Which didn't make it any different than any other company he'd worked for, but he wondered who started this one…that he was about to save their jobs.

Justin turned back to the cabinet and flipped through a file, glancing up for one more look at her. Ava pulled off wearing a suit like no woman he'd ever seen. Between the sexy way her hair looked piled on top of her head, and a slightly low-cut white blouse under her suit jacket revealing the top of her cleavage, he had to have her. Maybe he'd sneak her off to the broom closet when her meeting ended. Then again, she probably wouldn't appreciate getting dust all over her designer jacket.

What about the couch in his office? It never got much use, and maybe a healthy, heavy dose of sex with her would tide him over until that night.

Nah, he thought with a frown. He had to let her finish this project she'd been working so hard on. They only had a week left until the big night, and she deserved to give it her full attention. If it killed him, he'd make the sacrifice and leave her alone for a while.

Maybe after this project ended and life went back to normal for her they'd have more time together. Then reality hit. Who was he kidding? He and Ava would be a thing of the past, and he'd be in Miami trying to prove himself with another group of strangers.

Fielding walked past with Marshall Matheson, deep in conversation. Fielding glanced up. "Barrett, lunch tomorrow?"

Justin jumped back into work-mode and cleared this throat. He furrowed his brow, trying to look serious. "That works."

"Great," Fielding said. "Ali's. Across the street at one."

Justin nodded.

While the two execs returned to the conversation and headed further down the hall, Heather marched up to him, a stack of file folders in her arms. "Mr. Barrett, Mr. Fielding wants you to join the execs for a dinner party as his place tonight. I'll email you the directions." She passed him the folders. "And he wants an analysis of these before you leave tonight."

He took the files. "No problem. Thanks, Heather. Tell him I'm looking forward to the party."

But Fielding's assistant had already made her way toward the elevator. *Damn.* Party tonight? Some notice would have been good. Spur-of-the moment parties never fazed him before, so he figured he was losing his touch. So much for the night of raunchy Kama Sutra experiments with

Ava, but he knew using that as an excuse to Fielding wouldn't help either of them.

With one last look at Ava and a deep sigh, Justin headed back to his office with the stack of files.

In her office late that night, Ava finally looked up from her desk and realized she hadn't heard anyone walk past in hours. She peered out the door to discover the hallway lights off. She glanced around, searching for signs of life. Total silence.

Back in her office, she headed to the window and discovered that outside on crowded Melrose Avenue, traffic now flowed freely. She noticed the time on the wall clock and frowned. No wonder. Rush hour ended hours ago.

I'll go soon, she promised herself.

Ignoring the rumble in her stomach that reminded her she'd forgotten to eat again, she stepped out of her heels and held up a pair of red and white boxers with a hipster waist she'd just finished sewing. She dressed her favorite mannequin in them, and then set it beside the others lined up in front of her desk. They formed a nice, neat row of fake models of the male form.

She stepped back to review the day's work and folded her arms across her chest.

"Not too shabby, guys. What do you think?" she asked, beaming. She ran her hand over one of the mannequin's thongs and grinned at the expressionless face. "Do these work for you? They work for me." She plucked the elastic waistband and let it snap back.

Deciding she liked what she saw despite the lack of response from her inanimate men, she started cleaning up the mess of sewing supplies strewn across her desk. Working like a madwoman always resulted in thread, accessories, and scraps of fabric all over the place.

Her twelve-hour workday produced five new designs, and she wanted to see them finished and sewn before leaving for the day. She knew better than to ignore her muse when it kicked in full force, because who knew when it would show up again?

At this rate she'd have to cut the number of garments in the line down. She had thirty designs to fill twenty spots with, and more ideas in her head, ready to come out on paper.

She locked her sketches in one of her desk drawers and decided work was done for the night. She'd get back to it tomorrow, after some food and some rest.

She slipped into her heels, put her jacket back on, locked the office, grabbed her purse and portfolio, and headed down to the parking lot.

Despite her efforts and all her accomplishments today, one thing was missing. Looking at all those fake, plastic male bodies made her ache for one made of flesh. Come to think of it, ever since she'd met Justin, she had a permanent little ache in the pit of her stomach. A knot always formed when she didn't know when she'd see him next.

Just the thought of him excited her.

Still high on the thrill of creating something new, she thought about doing something crazy.

"Damn. Do you know how much that suit turns me on?" Justin leaned against the doorway frame, his arms folded across his chest, appraising Ava while she stood in the hall in front of his apartment.

If just the thought of him excited her, the sight of him standing there dressed in pants, his dress shirt unbuttoned at the top, bare feet, and a little grin on his face made her crazy. And the way he looked at her right now...she decided she liked his mouth falling open like that.

Carrying a paper bag full of Chinese food, she stepped inside. She set it on the dining room table with her purse while he shut the door. She turned to him. "Well, Mr. Barrett, do you prefer the suit on…or off?"

He scratched his chin, his eyes roaming up and down her body. "If you're gonna make me choose…"

"I am."

She loved the hazy look in his eyes.

He swallowed. "Off. Definitely."

She grinned with delight and stripped her jacket off. "That's what I was hoping."

Justin gave out a deep groan as he pulled her into his arms and brought his mouth to hers. This was too much fun, she thought, sinking her tongue between his lips. Her hands reached up to stroke his back, the clean smell of him invading her senses as she pressed her body to his, her breasts crushing against his chest.

"I love the way you kiss me," she murmured, her lips brushing across his.

"Yeah?" he asked, gently licking her upper lip with his tongue.

An ache between her thighs threatened to overtake her. "Mmmm…"

He sure made this whole seduction thing easy on a girl.

"Let's get you out of this," he said, reaching between them for the buttons of her blouse.

"You first." She unbuttoned his shirt, took it off, and tossed it onto a chair. Her hands moved over his warm flesh, feeling his hard muscled arms, the contours of his chest. She wrapped her arms around his neck, then leaned up on her tiptoes and pressed her mouth against his ear. "How about we give page thirty-six a try," she murmured.

She pulled away to catch his reaction.

He furrowed his brow, as if trying to remember which page that was. After a pause, his face brightened and he reached for her. "Hell, yeah."

"So you're up for the challenge?"

"Oh, I'm definitely up," he assured her.

While her mouth pressed against his again, she reached her hand down and pressed it against the hard length of him through his pants. She ran the tip of her tongue over her lips and smiled up at him. "Umm. So I see." She reached for the top button.

"Don't you want to talk first?" A mischievous twinkle appeared in his eye, giving his teasing away.

He unbuttoned her blouse and ran his fingers inside her bra, cupping one breast in his hand. "We could eat." He nodded toward the dining room table. "That food you brought smells really…" She reached inside his boxers, taking him in her hand, and he shut up. He squeezed his eyes shut and brushed his mouth against her hair.

She pulled the zipper of his jeans down, trying to push them around his hips.

While his fingers splayed across her, Justin's thumb stroked her hardening nipple. She drew in a little breath and pressed her mouth against his.

Stripping off her blouse, he revealed the sexy little white lace bra she'd designed one day at lunch that week.

His eyes roamed over her breasts. "What are you trying to do to me?"

Dropping to his knees, he slid the pantyhose down her legs. She shivered with delight as he planted little kisses on the flesh he slowly revealed.

"Step out." She obeyed the request and lifted one foot while he pulled the hose off one, then the other, while she balanced herself with her hands on his shoulders.

When she joined him on the floor he unhooked her bra, then kissed her breasts one by one. He palmed one while he drew the other in his mouth, teasing her with his tongue.

He slid her underwear off and turned her around, leaving her naked and alone on her hands and knees.

"Don't move."

Embarrassed at her awkward position, and frustrated at the loss of his touch, she looked back. "Justin, are you going to leave me like this?"

"Protection…" he mumbled, halfway across the room. "It's in the other…"

"In my purse," she said, trembling with anticipation while she waited.

"Sorry for the delay," he said a moment later, sidling up behind her. She noticed that he he'd also brought the Kama Sutra book. "Where were we?" he mumbled, flipping through the pages. She chuckled. How could he make her laugh despite the fact she felt as if she'd die if he didn't enter her that second?

She didn't have to wait much longer. He thrust into her, moving slowly at first, then increasing his pace while she moved with him. When he reached his hand around her belly and between her thighs, stroking her, she quaked and shook and couldn't stop herself from crying out.

He climaxed moments later, stilling inside her.

Ava sighed, collapsing on the floor, unable to prevent a grin from coming over her face. "I think I…like page thirty-six." She brushed a damp lock of hair away from her flushed face and tried to catch her breath.

Justin collapsed beside her. After a minute, he looked over at her and growled hungrily. "So. You ready for thirty-seven?"

Later, Ava lay on her side next to Justin, one leg hitched up over his. A couple of Chinese food containers lay empty on the nightstand in the dark bedroom. She lay her head down on the pillow, feeling sleepy and lazy and completely satisfied. She stroked Justin's torso, enjoying the feel of him under her hand. Very mysterious, this guy next to her. Somehow she'd discover all his little secrets.

Never in her wildest dreams had she thought anything would happen between them. Maybe this was a dream. Maybe she'd imagined this whole thing, and in reality she lived for designing full-coverage bloomers and bras, no man in sight.

But the very real male lying next to her told her otherwise. "I didn't mean for this to happen, you know," she murmured.

Justin ran a hand over his forehead. "Do you have any idea how glad I am you came over tonight? That boring dog and pony show at Fielding's house just about killed me."

She ran her lips across the faint trace of stubble on his chin. "I thought you liked those things."

He took a deep breath. "Only so much a guy can take."

"Really." Ava reached down between his thighs and caressed him, wrapping her fingers around him. She laughed. "You sure about that?"

He gave out a groan of pleasure. "You drive me crazy, you know that?"

"Mmmm…that's the idea," she replied. She moved her hand up and caressed his stomach, feeling the taut, warm muscles under her fingers. She settled her head against his chest.

"I thought about you all day."

She smiled, watching him. Her thoughts always ended up on him, too, despite trying to concentrate on her work. Truthfully, she thought about him all the time. "What did you think about?"

He turned to her. "Doing you on the couch in my office."

An incredulous grin came over her face. "Are you serious?"

"Dead."

Her cheeks flushed as an image of his little fantasy floated through her brain. "Mine might be more comfortable than yours."

"Want to try it tomorrow?" When she didn't answer, he laughed. "I'm not kidding."

She nudged his arm. "I'm serious, too. You know…I never planned for us to get involved like this."

He settled himself closer to her, wrapping one arm around her. "Me, either. You made me break my rule."

She lifted her head, fascinated. "What rule is that?"

"Never get involved with someone I work with."

Surprised, she stared at him. "You've never?"

He shook his head. "What about you?" He looked away. "Nah, don't tell me. I don't want to think about you with some other guy."

"Hmmm…would it make you jealous?" she asked.

His eyes met hers, the most serious look on his face she'd ever seen. "Yeah."

Melting, she put her chin on his chest and grinned. "So this rule of yours… does that mean Leslie never had a chance?"

He shook his head. "If you hadn't been irresistible…"

"I wouldn't have either, huh?"

She hoped this little thing they had going wasn't clouding his judgment. If he'd never done this before with someone he worked with, how would he know if she could really pull this off? Was it just because of what had happened between them?

"Justin, you're not doing this for me, are you? There's a rumor going around that you're keeping the company alive when it's falling apart. Do you really think we can pull Cupid's Beau off?"

"We? You're the one who's done the hard part."

"Do you think it'll work?"

"I know it will."

She thought about that. She wondered if anyone actually believed in her when they'd given her this project, or if they'd set her up for failure right from the start. It seemed like no matter what anyone else thought, though, she had Justin on her side. Justin. Still a mystery she intended to solve.

She leaned up on one elbow. "Justin?"

"Mmmm?"

"What were you like when you were younger?"

He shifted uncomfortably beside her. "What do you mean?"

"You never talk about your family."

"Not much family to talk about. I was an only child."

"Yeah, me, too, but…your parents, then. Where do they live?"

He sighed and fidgeted with the cup in front of him. "Uh…well…it's not that interesting. My story's not that great, believe me."

"I'd like to hear it," she murmured.

"Maybe later. I'm exhausted. Okay?"

Disappointed, she nodded. She didn't want to force it. But somehow…one day she'd get the truth out of him.

Justin stroked his hand across the softness of Ava's naked hip and watched her sleep. He'd never get enough of her, even if he had her a thousand times. Every time he made love to her he thought it would ease the ache inside him, and bring him closer to letting her go, but instead it just made him want her more.

He admired her more than anyone he'd ever met. He knew she had her doubts about herself, but he wasn't kidding thinking she could pull this off. Sell the company off piece by piece? Nah, that would be a waste. Not when she'd given something that would take them into next year and the years after that.

For once, he dedicated himself to the plan. He wasn't sure he could follow through, but for Ava, he'd give it his best shot.

Fielding poured himself a second glass of wine at Ali's Cafe the next afternoon. He tried to pour some in Justin's glass, but Justin covered it with his hand.

"Thanks, but…it's gonna be a long afternoon."

Fielding settled in his chair. "I need feedback on Cupid's Beau."

Justin savored a bite of shish kabob. "I reviewed the line so far. It looks incredible."

Fielding dipped a piece of pita bread into some hummus. "And the costs?"

"After careful research…I believe if we increase the units in the line…expand distribution by twenty percent…profits will soar."

Fielding raised one eyebrow. "Increase the units? Has Ms. Parker even completed the minimum yet?"

"She's well over the projected number of garments. I think when you see them, it'll be hard to exclude any from the line. Giving more choice to the customer will turn more of a profit overall."

Fielding shook his head and grimaced. "It's a risk."

"I've found some areas we can make cuts. That should help alleviate some risk if we increase production costs."

Fielding pursed his lips. After a long pause, he relaxed in the chair. "Sounds like you've done your homework."

Justin gave a wry smile. "I'm working on it."

"Look, we gave the line to Parker unsure of what the results would be. She was our best bet, but there was no guarantee…she's still a risk."

"That's what it's all about, isn't it?" Justin said, giving Fielding what his mother used to call his thousand-dollar smile.

Sure, she was a risk. When he first took this position he'd thought the company had set itself up for failure, but that was before he met Ava. Somebody knew what they were doing when they'd decided she was the one to take over Cupid's Beau.

Justin sliced into a grilled red pepper. "If you'd like to see a sample of what she's come up with, I'm sure I could persuade her to…"

"Tell her I'll need to see her samples this afternoon," Fielding replied. "But first, I want to know if *you* think she can pull this off."

"Thomas, I have no doubt that she will. Not only that, but we have a big surprise in store for you."

Fielding swallowed the last bite of pita bread and pursed his lips. "Glad you've been there to help her through this. Could have been a disaster. Hiring you was the best idea Matheson ever had," he growled under his breath.

Help Ava? Justin thought. Her name and "disaster" didn't belong in the same conversation. All he'd done was sit sat back…okay, all he'd done was *stand* there… naked…and watch her line come to life. Not a lot of effort on his part.

"She's done an amazing job all on her own."

"Don't be modest, Barrett. I heard that about you. Modest." His plate empty, Fielding wiped his mouth with a napkin and tossed it on the table.

Wait until the gala, Justin thought. It would be her night to finally show them all. He was sure after that they'd give her respect instead of torturing her, and she could work on that insecure thing she had going on, the one that didn't need to be there in the first place.

He sat back in his chair. Whether everyone admitted it or not, this project was Ava's and hers alone.

9

"*I'll* be right there. Yeah. Hang on, Mom."

Ava watched Justin fold up his cell phone and place it beside him in the jeep while they drove home from dinner in Santa Monica.

"Shit." He pressed the gas pedal hard.

Ava's heart started racing. Not like him to get upset about much of anything. She'd heard the stress in his voice during the call, and figured it must be something serious with his mom. "What's wrong?"

Justin headed toward the freeway entrance. He glanced over at her. "Do you mind going with me to the Valley? My mom got hurt and I need to check on her."

"Of course I don't mind. Is she all right? Should…should we call an ambulance or something?"

"I don't think so. She said she was cooking and cut herself with a knife. Said she's okay, but she gave herself a scare. I don't know, though. She doesn't usually call me unless she's in trouble."

"Where…where does she live?"

He sighed as he merged onto the freeway, focused on getting there. He cleared his throat. "Roscoe Hills."

She nodded. "Shouldn't take us long to get there."

Justin was silent, and feeling the tension in the air, Ava let him focus on driving, hoping everything would be okay once they got to his mother's house. They headed north on the freeway, way out into the Valley. In the silence, she secretly hoped she'd catch of glimpse of his old house, his old life. And the woman who gave birth to him might shed some light on him, she thought with a little smile. She hoped his mother was okay.

Justin finally pulled up into the driveway of a small, modest house at the end of a residential block. He undid his seatbelt and gave her a sheepish look. "Well, this is it."

She got out of the car and followed Justin as he rushed into the open front door of the house.

"Mom?" he called.

"I'm in the kitchen," a distraught female voice called.

A woman who could only be Justin's mother, dressed in a flowered robe with her hair in pink curlers, sat at the kitchen table, her hand resting in a red plastic bowl filled with ice water.

Justin rushed over to her. "What happened?"

"Just sliced my finger, is all. I was cutting up some veggies and the knife slipped." Her eyes brightened when she glanced up and noticed Ava. Her tone brightened. "Hello."

"Hi," Ava smiled.

"You didn't mention you were bringing a girlfriend over."

Justin cleared his throat, and Ava was surprised and the unusual look of embarrassment on his face. "Mom, this is Ava. Ava, this is my mom."

"Nice to meet you," Ava said shyly, noticing that his mother and Justin had the same dark hair and the same long, dark eyelashes. She recognized that full set of lips, too.

Justin nodded toward his mother's hand. "Did the bleeding stop?"

His mother pulled her hand from the bowl and examined her cut finger. "I think so."

Justin took her hand in his and examined it. "The cut's deep."

"It's not that bad. Not deep enough to need stitches."

"We should take you to the hospital, just to make sure."

"How many times did I take care of you when you got hurt? Trust me. I know when something needs stitches. I'm fine. I just…scared myself more than anything. I called you during the worst part. Just panicked, I guess."

"I can get some gauze or band-aids," Ava offered, trying to make herself useful.

"In the bathroom medicine cabinet, dear," his mother said.

Ava went down the hallway, returning to the kitchen with a package of band-aids and a small first aid kit. Justin opened the kit and washed her hands with some antiseptic, and then wrapped his mother's finger in some gauze.

"There, that's perfect," his mother said, examining her bandaged fingers. "Good as new."

"Does it hurt?" Justin asked.

"It's not that bad."

He stood up straight, his mouth forming a straight line. "I'll get you some aspirin."

"I already took two."

Ava looked on, touched by the attentive, gentle way Justin treated his mother while he looked her over. He looked so intense and worried about her.

"You two young people go on. I didn't realize I was interrupting your evening," his mother said, a sly smile coming across her face. "I'm glad to see that my son has someone…"

Justin put one hand on her shoulder. "You sure you're all right, Mom?"

"I'm fine. My poker friends are on their way." She patted her head. "Got to take these curlers out and get dressed."

"I could stay with you tonight…"

"Don't be ridiculous. Everything's fine. When I saw the blood I thought it was worse than it was and I needed you for moral support. You'd better go before they get here and rope you both into staying to play Texas Hold 'Em."

Justin gave Ava an uncertain look, and turned back at his mother. "My cell is on for the rest of the night. *All* night. If you need anything, and I mean anything, you call me. All right?"

"Okay."

"Promise me you'll call?"

"Yes. Now go on," she insisted, shooing them both out of the house.

"Nice to meet you, Mrs. Barrett," Ava said.

"Likewise, dear."

Justin gave her an embarrassed look while he grabbed the car keys out of his pocket. "You ready?"

She smiled. "Yeah."

Poker players parked on the street and headed up to his mother's house while Ava and Justin got back into the car.

"She's in for a fun night," Ava noted, turning back to watch them go inside.

"Yeah," Justin said, teeth gritted.

Justin drove Ava home without a word, and by the time he pulled the Jeep into her driveway, she couldn't stand the silence anymore.

"What's the matter?" she asked.

He walked with her to the front door. "Nothing. Everything's fine."

She gave him a knowing look. "No, it's not. You might as well tell me. You were fine until we got to your Mom's."

He still didn't respond.

She looked at him, frustrated. "Jus…"

He scuffed one foot on the sidewalk. Then he looked up at her. "Now you know."

She furrowed her brow, confused. "Know what?"

"What you asked me about the other night."

She shook her head. "I don't…"

"About my parents. I told you there wasn't much to tell. I told you the truth. There isn't much. My dad took off before I was born. Never met the guy. And that was my mom."

"Yeah. I'm glad I met her. She's nice…"

"She used to be really pretty."

Ava frowned. "She still is."

"I mean…yeah, she is, but…she used to take care of herself better. When she worked, she always tried to do herself up nicely. Make-up…her hair was nice. Seems like long time ago. I don't know when that stopped. Now she just…seems like she's given up."

"She looked fine to me, Justin…I don't think she's…"

"So now you know."

"I know what?"

"I've been pretending."

She took a deep breath. "Okay, I'm trying to figure this out, but I have to admit I'm a little confused here."

"Nothing confusing about it. I've been faking it all along. Only I guess I can't hide it from you anymore."

"Justin, what are you talking about? What are you hiding from me? What do you mean 'pretending'?"

"You know. Pretending to be this rich guy with everything going for him."

She tried to smile. "You *do* have everything going for you."

"But none if it's true. Well, tonight you saw the truth. That's where I came from. We lived in a trailer before she bought that house. That run-down, beaten up house that she refuses to leave." He shook his head, a disgusted look on his face.

She touched his arm, but he pulled away. "Justin…"

"Don't feel sorry for me."

"Why would I do that?"

"Because of what you saw. I know you must think…that…"

"How do you know what I think?"

He gave her a guilty look.

She took his face between her hands, examining his sheepish expression. "I don't feel one bit sorry for you. Why should I? Or your mom. She seems like an amazing, proud woman. So what if she doesn't have a fancy house? She knows what's important."

"Yeah…" he muttered.

"She raised *you*, didn't she?" Ava started walking toward the front door without him. "If you ask me, you turned out pretty well."

"Where are you going?" he called after her.

"I can't believe you," she said, disbelief in her voice.

"Why?"

"Is that why you wouldn't tell me anything about your mom? Because of her house and where she lives? Because she doesn't have a lot of expensive stuff? What, did you think I'd judge you?"

He shrugged. "I…"

"Did you?"

After a moment, Justin shrugged and looked at her.

Ava let out a sigh. "After all we've been through…"

"I didn't grow up like you, Ava. My mom wasn't starring in TV shows and buying nice clothes.

Ava shook her head, giving him a look like she couldn't believe he just said that. She started walking away again.

"She worked in a diner so she could put food on the table. I started working when I was fourteen to help out."

"You're just digging yourself deeper, Justin."

"Wait…"

She turned around, her eyes meeting his. "And you think that any of this would have mattered to me?"

He took her arm. "How could it not?"

She rolled her eyes.

"I'm serious. How could it not? You think your mom would want you hanging out with someone like me?"

She yanked her arm away. "What, so now my mom's shallow, too?"

"That's not…what I meant," he murmured.

"I don't care how much money your mom had…or has. And I don't care where you grew up. And I can't believe you think I'd judge you for it." She stormed away from him.

"Ava, wait. Come back here…"

She stopped and turned to face him.

"I wasn't saying you're shallow. That's not how I wanted it to come out. Look, it's my issue…I'm the one who's ashamed of it."

She took a step closer. "What do you have to be ashamed of?"

He shrugged.

"Well…stop being ashamed."

He nodded, as if thinking about it. "Easier said than done."

"I'm sure you'd done harder things."

"I didn't mean to insult you, Ava. Like I said. It's my issue."

"Well, get over it."

He pondered that for a minute, and then gave her a half-grin, trying to break the tension. "I like it when you get all demanding."

She couldn't help but smile a little. After a moment, she added, "Promise me you'll try."

"Yeah. I guess…I guess I can do that."

"Good. I think that's a great idea. Because your mom's amazing." She stopped to give him a shy, little smile before she wrapped her arms around him. "And so are you."

"Now you know about me," he said. He wrapped his arms around her and pulled her up against him. "You know the truth."

She leaned in and planted a kiss on his lips. A grin came over her face when she rubbed her cheek against his. "Good."

"Get your hide in here *now*. I want to meet this guy," an irritated Charlotte said on the other end of the phone.

"We're coming," Ava replied. She flipped her cell shut and stuffed it in her purse, then turned to Justin while they walked down Melrose toward The Bungalow Club for Charlotte's party. "I think she's drunk already."

With a shrug, Justin grinned. "It *is* her birthday."

When they reached the outside of the club, Ava took a deep breath and grabbed Justin's hand for moral support. "You sure you're ready for this?" she asked.

The picture of confidence, he replied, "Sure." He squeezed her hand. "You?"

"Yeah," she muttered. *Liar.* She couldn't remember the last time she'd introduced someone she was dating to her friends, and she wasn't sure how they'd react.

Justin, however, looked perfectly at ease as they strode inside the crowded bar area toward the outdoor back patio.

Cabanas surrounded the perimeter, with open tables in the middle. Heat lamps warmed the cool night air, and white candles cast a soft glow over the patio area.

At their reserved cabana table, Charlotte jumped up from her chair when she saw them.

"Ava!" Charlotte brought them both over to the table. "Here she is. Everyone, this is Justin. Justin, this is Danni and Rick, Kristin and Adam, and this is Stefanie." She grinned. "And I'm Charlotte."

"The birthday girl." Justin's smile widened as he shook her hand.

Charlotte giggled, her cheeks reddening.

Justin exchanged pleasantries with her friends while Charlotte motioned a server toward them. She pointed to Justin and Ava. "Excuse me, can we get these two a drink?"

But the server rushed past without hearing her.

"I'll take care of it," Justin volunteered. He turned to Ava. "What are you having?"

"A martini?" Ava replied, hoping it would calm her down a little.

He nodded and turned to her friends. "Anyone else want anything?"

Everyone shook their heads, the girls staring at Justin with fascination.

Before heading off to get drinks, Justin gave Ava a little kiss on the cheek. "Be right back."

Ava hugged Charlotte. "Happy Birthday."

"Birthday-Schmirthday. How did you forget to mention that he's *gorgeous*?" Charlotte demanded, pushing Ava away.

"And a gentleman," Stefanie pointed out, raising her half-full margarita glass for emphasis.

"Go, Ava," Danni said, taking a sip of beer. "So that's why we haven't seen you lately."

Ava blushed and sat down. "You guys…"

"Come on now, you've been holding out on us long enough. We want every hot detail," Danni said, devouring a shrimp appetizer.

"Give her a break," Rick said, leaning back comfortably in his chair.

"Yeah," Adam agreed.

"No," Danni insisted, glaring at her boyfriend. "She's been AWOL for over a month."

Charlotte grabbed a tiny pizza appetizer that just arrived at their table. "She's got a big project at work that's keeping her busy."

Danni nodded in Justin's direction before grabbing another shrimp. "Yeah. I'll just bet," she said dryly.

Charlotte gently elbowed Danni and shot her a look, while Ava laughed to herself. She loved it when they talked about her like she wasn't there.

Justin returned with drinks and sat down between Ava and Charlotte.

"So…Justin. How'd you get Ava to go out with you?" Charlotte asked, downing the rest of her beer.

Ava wanted to cover her face with her hands and crawl underneath the table. *Here we go. The humiliation begins.*

"Yeah," Kristin asked, leaning in closer.

All of a sudden, all eyes were on Justin.

Danni nudged her. "That was kind of rude, Charl," she whispered.

Charlotte's face turned red. "Ha! I didn't mean it like that! I just mean that she…ah…" She sighed and slumped in her chair. "You all know what I mean."

Justin grinned at Ava. "Well, it wasn't easy."

"She never is," Stefanie laughed.

Ava gave her friend a look that said *shut up*.

"I guess you could say…I wore her down," Justin said. "It took a while, but she finally agreed to have dinner with me one night…and…" He grabbed Ava's hand. "The rest is history."

"Wow," Stefanie said, like that was the most romantic story in the world.

"Come on, you had to have gone through more than that to get her," Kristin said, frowning.

With a huge grin on her face, Charlotte nudged Ava's arm. "So much for your plan to stay an old maid, huh?"

"I had a plan?" Ava asked innocently.

"Come on, don't you remember in eighth grade when you had a crush on Derek Larston?" Charlotte asked.

Ava rolled her eyes. "Do we have to go there?" she asked through gritted teeth.

"When he started going out with Kelly instead of you, you told us you were bound to wind up an old maid."

"And we've been calling her that behind her back ever since," Danni told Justin.

"Really," Justin said, fascinated, his eyes bright.

"She even started designing her underwear wardrobe to match that image," Charlotte said. "As I'm sure you know."

"Okay, that's it. No more talk about my underwear," Ava laughed, dying for this conversation to be over.

"Justin, what do you do?" Charlotte asked.

More appetizers arrived at the table.

Kristin turned to Rick. "Did you order these?"

"I was hungry," he replied, grabbing an egg roll.

Kristin shrugged and took one.

"I, uh…I'm a consultant…for a lot of different companies," Justin replied, helping himself to an egg roll, too.

"Do you like it?"

He gave them a smile. "It keeps me moving around a lot. And it keeps my skills sharp."

Justin quickly changed the subject off of work. Everyone demanded to know more about how he'd gotten together with Ava. She hoped he wouldn't reveal too many embarrassing details, but he remained the gentleman and very elusive about certain things. He kept the conversation moving from movies, to outdoor activities, to sports. Ava relaxed, just as fascinated with Justin as her friends seemed to be.

The party kept going until after two a.m. when the club closed.

Ava sighed with relief when it was time to go, but more from wanting to get Justin all to herself than the fact that she was tired.

When everyone finally split up, Charlotte pointed to Justin. "You take care of Ava."

"Will do," he said.

"See you tomorrow, Charlotte," Ava said, giving her a hug. "We'll fit that bra for your dress."

"Yeah. I can't wait to see this," Charlotte joked, adjusting her bosom.

Later, Justin lay in Ava's bed, waiting for her to join him. He looked around her bedroom, leaning back against the comfortable down pillows. He liked this place. He'd spent less and less time at his sterile, almost empty corporate apartment the last few weeks, preferring to be here with her whenever he got the chance.

He was glad she'd invited him to the party. He'd gotten proof of what he suspected all along: Ava had real friends who accepted her for who she was. Those people had known everything about her since eighth grade, the fantastic parts and the embarrassing parts, and he wondered what that would be like. Hell, when he'd escaped from middle school, he never looked back. But what he wouldn't give to have what she'd had. To have someone know and accept him like that.

He looked up to find Ava silhouetted in the doorway. If she could look any sexier in her tiny little nightgown, he had no idea how. She came in holding the Kama Sutra book with both hands against her chest, and then offered it to him.

She grinned and climbed onto the bed, straddling his lap. He sighed. *Finally.* He'd wanted to get her on top of him all night.

"What page do you want to do?" she asked.

She waited with an expectant look on her face. After a minute, Justin took the book, and then tossed it onto the nightstand. He reached for her. "How about we make up our own variation?"

She nodded. "That would be…" She gasped when his hand slid up her thigh and underneath the nightgown. "Um…good."

He loved it when he got her excited. Loved her little sighs of pleasure and the way her cheeks flushed and how her breath started coming faster. He pulled the nightgown over her head, and then rolled her over until she lay beneath him. "You've known everyone at the party tonight since eighth grade?" He settled himself on top of her.

"*First* grade, actually." She stroked her hands along his sides and added affectionately, "And every one of them is a pain in the butt."

"They adore you."

She laughed. "No, I think they adore *you*."

Justin wrapped his arms around her, never more content in his life. He loved the way she felt. He loved…her? Nah, he couldn't go there.

Damn. They were good together, in every way he could think of. He'd wanted to tell her he was leaving, but as he leaned down and brought his mouth to hers, he knew he couldn't bring himself to do it tonight.

Charlotte emerged from Ava's bedroom wearing her blue bridesmaid's dress with the strapless bra Ava had made for her underneath. She twirled around for inspection. Which meant she couldn't have had that much of a hangover from her birthday party. *Good.*

"My sister has no taste," Charlotte said, examining the ruffles on the bottom.

"She went for…flamboyant," Ava said hopefully.

"I would have settled for simple and elegant," Charlotte huffed. "Does the bra show anywhere?" she asked, peeking down at her cleavage.

Sitting comfortably on her blue denim couch, Ava shook her head. "How does it fit?"

Charlotte smoothed her hands over her dress. "The dress…aside from being ugly, okay. The bra…perfect."

"Shift around some. Does it itch or anything? Ride up?"

Charlotte moved her shoulders around, and then shook her head. "It's so comfortable! I've never had a bra fit like this."

"Good." Ava smiled to herself, thinking about the efforts she'd gone to before Charlotte finally agreed to give her a chance to make her this bra. It didn't hurt that their shopping trip left them empty handed and Charlotte was desperate, but Ava knew all along her friend would be happy with the end result.

"Hey, how'd you whip this up so fast when you've got that big presentation coming up?"

Ava shrugged, unable to hold back a secretive little smile. "The muse has been good to me lately."

"I want to give you money for this…"

"What?" Ava gave her friend a look like she'd gone crazy. "Don't be silly. I'm not taking your money."

Satisfied that she had a happy customer, she packed a few sewing supplies back in her bag.

"I'm serious," Charlotte protested, fooling around with the top of the dress. "You saved me. Don't know what I would have done for this wedding. No store sells anything that works with this crazy dress my sister picked out, and those pasty things you stick on your boobs don't work too well." She sighed. "Believe me, I've tried."

She turned and held her arms up, and Ava took it as her cue to help unzip the dress.

"So…does your muse just happen to have dark hair, dark eyes, look sexy in black pants, and have a killer smile?" Charlotte turned around to get a reaction.

Ava blushed and couldn't help grinning while she unzipped the dress. "Maybe."

"Are you guys…uh, serious?"

She thought about that. Truthfully, the question crossed her mind every hour. "Well, we both have a lot going on. We haven't had much of a chance to talk about it. Why?"

Charlotte bit her lower lip, and between that and her silence, Ava spotted trouble right away.

She cocked her head. "What is it, Charl? Come on, out with it."

Charlotte plopped down on the couch. "You look fantastic together…"

Ava gave her a knowing look. "But…?"

"Are you sure this guy isn't going to break your heart?"

Ava grabbed a welted pillow from the couch and hugged it tightly against her chest. She furrowed her brow. She'd thought about that some, but she'd been having too much fun to pay any attention to her doubts. "How would I know that?" she asked softly.

"I suppose there's never any guarantee, but you don't seem like the type who'd fool around forever without potential for something else. And I don't know if he's the kind of guy…"

"To be serious?"

"Yeah."

Now this was getting interesting. She'd caught Charlotte talking alone with Justin last night, so she must have gotten to know him a little. She might as well get her friend's honest opinion. Ava had been so deep in this that maybe she couldn't see it for what it was.

"So you don't think he's serious about me."

"It's pretty obvious he's in to you, but something makes me think…"

Ava tossed the pillow aside and sighed deeply. "What?"

"He just doesn't seem like your type…"

"I have a type?"

Holding the dress up around her chest, Charlotte headed into the bedroom. "We just picture you with someone more stable."

"You guys discussed this, then."

"We're just not sure that he's the kind of guy who'll stick around." A minute later Charlotte emerged from the bedroom in a T-shirt, buttoning up a pair of jeans. "That's just the impression I got. And he said himself he moves around a lot. Look, it doesn't take a lot to see that you care about him, and I don't want him leaving you with a broken heart."

Ava stood up and starting pacing. "I've always thought he was out of my league. We *are* really different. Maybe I've been kidding myself that this can work."

But Charlotte didn't know what happened after they'd gotten home last night. He couldn't have made love to her the way he did and not mean it. Could he?

"Look, we're really happy for you. Maybe it'll be great, and we hope it is. The last thing we all want is for you to get hurt. That's all."

"And you think I *will* get hurt," Ava murmured, collapsing onto the couch.

Charlotte sat down beside her. "Just be careful, okay?"

10

Making her way through twenty models getting ready for the gala in the back room of the Beverly Hilton, Ava watched them dress at their stations, comb their hair, and check themselves out in the full-length mirrors.

The moment she'd worked for had almost arrived, and her stomach cramped. She wondered if the guys were as nervous as she was. If *anyone* else was this nervous.

Underwear had been her life ever since she could remember. No matter who laughed at her, or ridiculed her work through the years, she always thought one day she'd make a name for herself, and finally get a little respect. *I deserve that, don't I?* She'd grown the last few weeks, and pulled off something she didn't think she'd ever be able to do. The thought of all of her hard work being on display for everyone to see made her nervous and a little self-conscious.

She caught a glimpse of herself and smoothed down the skirt of her black dress. Not too bad, she thought, shifting around on her new pair of spiky black heels.

No one could accuse her of not putting out any effort tonight. During the week, she'd treated herself to a facial and a French manicure, and then headed to Melanie's Boutique to spoil herself rotten. She'd tossed out what little make-up she had lying around her house, and started fresh at the make-up counter. She spent three hours with a consultant named Rita who'd shown her how to glam herself up, and Ava had walked out with over three hundred dollars of designer supplies. She'd done a few test runs with her hair throughout the week, and decided to style it in an elegant up-do with a few tendrils curling loose around her face. A new pair of earrings and necklace completed the outfit.

Pleased with the way she'd put herself together for her big event, she stepped away from the mirror.

Wearing nothing but a G-string, Mr. Rhinestone came over and gave her the once-over. "Wow, you look…" He nodded his approval. "Uh…" He glanced downward. "Ms. Parker…Ava…can you take a look and let me know how this fits?"

Forced to examine his crotch to see how the red thong fit, all the blood rushed to her face and she knew it must have turned fifteen shades of crimson.

"Uh…it looks good. Very good."

"Great." He winked at her, and then strutted back to his dressing table.

Still grinning with embarrassment, she shook her head. What a crazy job she'd gotten herself into.

She clapped her hands, quieting everyone, and then announced over the chaos, "Gentlemen, before you put your pants on…I want to do a thorough…"

The models lined up for her inspection before she'd finished her request. She grinned to herself. *If my friends could see me now.*

She appraised their skivvies one by one and beamed. Each and every guy looked perfect.

"Now remember…"

"Wait until the lights go up to drop our pants," announced a chorus of deep male voices.

"Yes. Perfect." She took a breath. They'd practiced it several times in rehearsal last night to perfect the timing, but with a room full of people, the unpredictable loomed in the background.

Figuring there wasn't much more she could do, she thumbed toward the exit. "Guess I'll…just…be outside."

She figured they were capable of putting on their tuxes without her help.

Heading outside, she peeked into the gala area and noticed a line of guests filing in.

Thirty tables were set with designer china and silverware, with champagne glasses made of the finest crystal. Tiny red hearts covered the top of the white linen tablecloths, and little white lace-covered boxes of chocolate tied with a red bow on each person's plate completed the place settings. A huge red heart hung from the podium set up in front for Fielding to announce the event.

Ava smiled with anticipation. *Simple, elegant…perfect.* The room looked just how she'd planned: like a Valentine's Day paradise.

When she felt a hand go around her waist and pull her around, she squealed. A surge of delight went through her heart at the sight of Justin. She'd kept her distance this week, and he'd let her, saying he knew how busy she was. She'd refused his help and he'd let her do her thing. She'd digested what Charlotte said and wasn't sure how she felt about it.

He rushed her down a hallway and pulled her into his arms, and she couldn't resist wrapping her arms around his waist. He felt even better than he looked.

He held her at arm's length, hungry eyes roaming over her. "You look…"

"Yes?" she asked, grinning with anticipation.

He licked his lips. "I…uh…I'm…"

Her grin widened. "Speechless?"

He nodded. "That dress…"

Looking up at him through her lashes, she asked, "You like it?"

"Oh, yeah." He dragged her up against him.

"Mmmm." She leaned in to press her mouth against his. "I'm so glad you're here."

"Damn. Wish Fielding hadn't put us at opposite ends of the room." He leaned closer and murmured, "I missed you this week."

She nodded. "Me, too." Staying away had been torture, and despite her doubts sinking in, she'd had a little knot in the pit of her stomach without him.

"What do you say we have our own little private celebration later?" he asked quietly.

She opened her mouth to respond, but before she could, he kissed her, one hand on her back, steadily making its way downward. He grabbed her ass, and then pulled her leg up around his hip.

"Justin, you're going to mess up my dress," she protested, laughing softly.

"Want me to stop?"

She bit her lower lip, contemplating. "Well…maybe not yet."

But he let her go anyway. "You nervous?" he asked.

"A little," she nodded, the relaxed grin on his face calming her down.

"It's gonna go great."

"I think it's out of my hands now." She reached up and played with his tie. "Guess I'd…better check on the models and get them out there."

"Can't wait till you stop hanging out with all those other guys."

She grinned. "Won't be long, now. After tonight, I'm all yours."

"I like that." His thumb brushed over her cheek. "Good luck."

She nodded, and with one last kiss, he took off.

The room where the guys had dressed had emptied out. She headed into the gala area, which was filled with music, conversation, and laughter while the guests sat down. The waiters took orders, the situation well under control. The guys looked fabulous, and she smiled, thinking of the secret entertainment to come.

Throughout the evening, guests feasted on a choice of filet mignon or rigatoni and sautéed vegetables, with a variety of white wines. Ava glanced around, recognizing two fashion editors sitting at one of the tables across from her. A buyer from a department store sat at a table in the corner, laughing with another prestigious buyer she recognized. She gulped. *No pressure or anything.*

After dinner died down, the lights dimmed, leaving candles in the middle of the tables to cast a soft glow over the guests. Ava heard the gasps and "oohs", and looks of anticipation on their faces. When the lights came up again, the music switched to a sexy, seductive song, and the twenty waiters simultaneously began their striptease.

They started off slow, removing their bowties and tossing them aside. Next, they slid their black jackets over their shoulders and let them fall to the ground. In unison, they unbuttoned their white tuxedo shirts button by button. When the last button was open, they eased the shirts off, revealing a set of tanned, muscular male torsos.

Ava's breath caught in her throat waiting for the big moment.

All together, moving as one to the music, the waiters unzipped, then dropped their pants, revealing her designs underneath.

She glanced around, noticing several jaws dropping to the floor.

Then all at once, the room erupted in thunderous applause, cat-calls, and shouting. All the adrenaline left her body in a flood of relief.

Mr. Rhinestone grabbed the microphone off the podium. His deep voice boomed through over the music as he announced, "Ladies and gentlemen…Skiv-Ease's new Cupid's Beau line!"

The audience applauded again. The tension in the hall dissolved as the models paraded toward the raised stage for everyone to view the complete collection from the front. Then they spun around for a back view.

After everyone got a good view of the "official" presentation, they returned to mingle amongst the tables of guests, serving tarts and chocolate mousse in their skivvies. Some people laughed, some watched the models with disbelief.

Ava caught one woman staring at Mr. Rhinestone's butt.

"And what are these made of, young man?" the woman asked.

"Silk," he proudly announced, strutting over to another group of groping females.

"Are they for sale?" she called after him.

Mr. Rhinestone pointed toward a small table, where Heather took underwear orders for guests. Ava followed his gaze with her own and noticed that the "buy" line went out the door. *Wow.*

And Justin couldn't have looked more at home working the room, drinking champagne and talking to Marshall Matheson and Colin Sheppard. She saw Fielding slap his shoulder a couple of times. She'd never seen the boss so happy, or the board members so animated. She inched closer to get a better look.

"I know you said you had a surprise in store, but I never expected *that!*" Fielding laughed, slapping Justin on the back. "I knew you had it in you, but I never thought we'd get a response like this. Look around. Who would have thought all these buyers would jump at this…we're going all out." He leaned closer, roughly massaging Justin's shoulder with one hand.

No doubt about it, Ava thought. The usually standoffish executive had to be drunk.

Fielding glanced around the room, watching the buyers. He nodded with approval. "We put on a pretty good show tonight. Your reputation preceded you, Barrett, but I can't believe you pulled this off." He laughed, elbowing Justin's arm. "Don't take that the wrong way."

Ava headed toward them, but instead of noticing her, Fielding turned to an executive Ava recognized from some of their meetings with

Krombar, an International Department store.

Fielding slapped him on the shoulder. "Bierlich, you old coot, who would have thought you'd show up here tonight?"

Just as Bierlich opened his mouth to reply, a huge group of executives and their guests gathered around Justin and Fielding. Ava couldn't hear anything through the deep masculine laughter.

A group of models came up to Ava. Before she could protest, Mr. Rhinestone and Carlos Mizero lifted her up.

She squealed and laughed as they carried her around the room chanting, "For she's a jolly good fellow...for she's a jolly..."

"Put me down!" she laughed.

She looked up just in time to catch Fielding practically shoving Justin out the front door, a crowd following after them.

Later, Ava headed outside the hotel, wondering where everyone went.

Her cell phone rang in her purse, making her jump. She took it out and answered it.

"Where are you?" Justin asked, a cacophony of noise in the background.

"Outside the hotel."

"I saw those guys kidnap you while Fielding took me away. You okay?"

"Sure...where are you?"

"London Jungle. Get your gorgeous self over here."

London Jungle was always a scene. She sighed. "I don't know if I'm up for it."

"You earned this. Now get your sweet little butt over to the bar. Don't make me do this alone. I'll be waiting," he said.

Before she could protest, Justin hung up.

London Jungle turned out to be packed, and Ava noticed that the rest of the employees from Skiv-Ease, including Leslie and Derek, had joined the party. Everyone gathered around Justin at the bar area, where he worked the crowd. Male and female alike, people fawned over him, loved him everywhere he went. How did he make it look so easy?

Ava watched Fielding's drink spill from his martini glass as he held it up. "A toast! To the man of the hour."

"Hear, hear!" groups of voices shouted in unison.

"To Justin. Who made tonight the greatest night of Skiv-Ease's year."

Everyone raised their glasses and drank to Justin's success.

A chant started somewhere in the crowd and wouldn't let up. "Speech, speech, speech!"

"All right, all right." Laughing, Justin motioned for everyone to stop.

The voices gradually died down.

He amazed her. He made people laugh, made them comfortable, made them feel like they were something special to be getting his attention. And she noticed his flushed cheeks, something she'd only seen after he'd had a little too much to drink.

"It's been a fantastic couple of months, everyone," Justin began. "Making this line come to life…"

"Literally!" someone yelled, and everyone cracked up.

"Uh, yeah." Justin cleared his throat with a good-natured laugh. "Literally. Getting to this point tonight was a rough road. But all the hard work finally paid off. It's been great working with all of you, and I want to thank everyone for your help. I didn't do this alone. And…the person I most want to thank, the woman who put this entire thing together…Ava Parker. Ava, come on up here."

Ava's cheeks flushed as she headed up to stand beside Justin. To her amazement, everyone applauded, cheers reverberating through the bar area. "This woman tirelessly designed every pair of underwear you saw tonight. She put tonight together and I want everyone to see how amazing she is."

"A-va! A-va!" a few guys yelled out.

Catcalls followed.

She hadn't realized how much getting recognition embarrassed her. She wasn't used to it, that was for sure.

"I'm sorry to announce that my time at Skiv-Ease is coming to an end," Justin continued.

"No!" protested several scantily clad and very drunk Skiv-Ease women, falling over one another.

"I'm headed for my next job in Miami next week…"

Ava's head shot up while the crowd groaned in protest. She stared at him, mouth agape, to make sure she'd heard him right. *Miami?* What was he talking about?

"You can't move away and leave us!" one of the women slurred.

Justin laughed.

Ava stood there, paralyzed. She tried to back away from him, but couldn't seem to make any of her body parts move. Tears welled up in her eyes. *He has to be kidding around, right? He would have told me first.*

"But I wanted to let you all know how great it's been working with everyone at Skiv-Ease, and thanks for helping make tonight the success that it was. I wish you all the best of luck."

Justin raised his beer glass.

"Good luck!" everyone called out, raising their glasses along with him. Several people swooped in and surrounded him, and the crowd continued to mingle.

Dazed, Ava slowly made her way toward the door.

"Parker!"

Ava turned around to find Leslie running up after her. She fought back a bout of tears.

"You did well, Parker," Leslie said.

Derek rushed up to join them. "I have to hand it to you, Ava. You pulled this off."

Several other employees gathered around them, congratulating her.

"Thanks," Ava said, her eyes welling up. Once upon a time she would have been flabbergasted at the recognition. Now she couldn't be happy for what she'd waited so long for and finally received. Not when Justin made that announcement. She forced a smile, and turned away so they wouldn't see her cry. "If you'll excuse me..."

She rushed off to get outside before she burst into tears.

Justin laughed and drank and had a good time at the bar. Wasn't this what he craved? Getting all the attention, getting to play hero? His time at Skiv-Ease was almost over. And it felt good. Wasn't the plan to stay unattached and move on? He'd proven himself, and there wasn't much more to be done. Soon he'd be out of here and on to the next assignment, just like he'd planned. *Worse things than drinking and hanging out on Miami Beach, right?*

But lately, being charming and wonderful, something that normally came easily, had expended a lot of energy. It had gotten harder and harder to maintain his façade, and he'd wanted to give his energy to other things. Like being with Ava every chance he got, spending every second he could with her.

He wondered how he'd pull off leaving, but in the long run, it was the right thing to do. Who was he kidding, thinking maybe he and Ava had some sort of future. They couldn't make this work. He wasn't a "make it work" kind of guy. That took sticking with something...or someone, and that wasn't exactly his specialty. Long term anything didn't work for him.

Through the crowd, he saw Ava slinking off toward the front door without a word to anyone. *Where is she going?*

Shit. Was he stupid? Before he'd realized what he was saying, he told everyone he was leaving for Miami before he'd bothered to tell her. This wasn't the way he pictured her finding out.

He'd wanted to tell her the night of Charlotte's party, but he couldn't bring himself to do it. How could he look at her and think about going anywhere without her? He couldn't deal with it. Instead, he'd decided to announce it to everyone else while she stood there and listened. *Coward.*

No matter what his future plans held, tonight was supposed to be her night, and he wasn't about to let her get away that easily.

Ava made her way outside, nearly tripping over her own feet in her high heels. She'd gotten what she wanted: recognition. And it didn't mean a whole lot when her heart felt like it would burst out of her chest any second.

She stuffed her hand in her purse searching for the valet parking stub. She planned to get the car as fast as she could and take off. Drained and exhausted, she felt unbelievably stupid on top of it. All this time she'd been kidding herself about Justin.

Just like that, they were finished.

He'd been using her. He'd used her to get a few hot and sexy underwear designs, and some convenient sex. The plan had always been to head off to Miami Beach when the job ended, leaving her hurt and alone. Did he think that's all she wanted from him?

She cursed herself for getting her feelings mixed up in this and caring about him. For thinking for one second that he cared about her.

She'd been lost in her own hopes that her feelings might be mutual, even though they hadn't discussed exactly what he wanted from her. This is exactly what Charlotte tried to warn her about.

Did a single night she and Justin spent together mean anything?

She wanted to throw her Kama Sutra books away, along with every reminder she had of him.

Panicking, she tried to come up with a plan to forget about this and make things go back to normal. She'd go home and rest, and when she got up in the morning…alone…she'd go about her business the way she did before she met him. She'd get groceries, clean the house, work, and her life would go on just as it always had.

When she turned around to find Justin running after her, she picked up her pace.

"Ava…wait," he called. "Would you just wait? Slow down."

She stopped and turned.

He'd caught up to her, his tie loosened and the sleeves of his dress shirt rolled up. "Where're you going?"

"Home. Where do you think?"

His eyes pleaded with her. "Come on, don't leave like this."

"What do you expect? You think I want to spend another second in there?"

"Everyone loved you…"

"I don't care. It doesn't matter." She sniffed while she raised her chin up. Her eyes bored into his. "Shouldn't you be out making moving plans?"

He lowered his head. "Look, I'm sorry I didn't tell you," he said quietly. "Sorry you had to find out like this."

"You're…sorry? That's all I get?" She gulped, hoping that would keep her from bursting into tears.

"Shit," he muttered, scrubbing his furrowed brow.

Her chest hurt as she tried to keep from crying. "You…didn't even have the courtesy to tell me before you announced it to everyone at the bar?"

He looked confused. "I…"

So much for playing it cool. She could feel big fat, hot tears running down her cheeks. She sniffled. "So…this whole thing, this whole time, you were using me. Just to get some underwear designs out of me."

A pained expression came over his face. "No…"

Unable to keep it in anymore, she gave out a little sob. "You know, Justin, you could have just told me what you wanted the underwear to look like. You didn't have to make it so complicated for yourself. I might have been able to come up with some good stuff without you having to spend time with me, *without* having to sleep with me. I am *insane* to think I meant anything to you, aren't I?"

"Ava…"

She headed for the stand and gave the valet her ticket. "After everything that's happened, you couldn't even tell me what your plans were?"

"I wanted to tell you."

"That's not an excuse, Justin! You weren't ever going to tell me, were you? I think you were going to disappear as quietly as you came in. But only after you got what you wanted, right? Another successful assignment. And I was just helping you get it."

"That's not…"

"This was my fault, too, though, wasn't it? I was stupid enough to think you might have felt something for me. That we might have had something. What an idiot, huh?"

The valet pulled her car up and she climbed inside.

"Ava, would you give me a chance to…"

"You had your chance."

She shut the car door quietly, so he wouldn't see how she really felt, and headed onto Santa Monica Boulevard without looking back.

Didn't seem fair for Justin to see how much he'd upset her, when clearly, she didn't mean a thing to him.

11

Justin surveyed the crowd surrounding him at The Pelican, an outdoor bar on South Beach. He'd tried to appreciate the twenty-four hour party, but the festive Saturday night atmosphere and the reggae music didn't do anything to cheer him up. Nothing had improved his mood since his arrival in Miami two weeks before.

A long, lit-up counter surrounded an island with hundreds of bottles of alcohol. Patrons filled every stool, and the standing room only crowd pressed up behind him. His coworker Chad, and Chad's scantily clad girlfriend Eden, sat on either side of him.

"I had to get this guy out," Chad yelled to Eden over a particularly loud Bob Marley song. "Working twelve hours every day without a break…got a lot more stamina than me." He raised his beer glass.

Eden gave Justin a look somewhere between admiration and wonder as she sipped her banana daiquiri. "Are you serious? You work that hard?"

Chad patted Justin on the back. "He just doesn't quit. Saved my ass this week, too, with that financial analysis he came up with."

Justin ground his teeth. Why should he take credit for working intense twelve-hour days at TimeSpace Management when he only did it to keep his mind off of other things? Not like he'd enjoyed it. And he hadn't enjoyed trying to prove himself…again…to people he'd never see again after his assignment ended.

Eden leaned in close and batted her eyelids. "You sound like a hard worker."

"Yeah, well…that's why they pay me the big bucks," Justin said under his breath, and downed the last sip of his drink.

Chad took one of the next round of beers that arrived, and set the other in front of Justin. "Don't be so modest."

Justin wrapped his hands around the cold glass. Two weeks down, a month and a half to go. Then he'd head to Entertech in Atlanta, leaving all this behind. No need to make any real connections here, but he figured it wouldn't kill him to hang out.

"Where are you staying?" Eden asked.

"Windsor Corporate on the beach."

She nodded. "Sounds nice."

Justin had to admit that the place had a great view, and all the necessities. But the smell of cleaning solution, bare walls, and the ugly black leather couch didn't exactly make it feel like home. For the first time, he wished he could pick his own place instead of having some company pick it for him.

Eden flipped a lock of long blond hair over her shoulder. "I have so many friends I want to set you up with." She looked at Justin, a flirtatious smile on her face. "Seriously, they're going to go crazy for you."

"Uh…I won't be in town that long," Justin warned.

Eden gave him a seductive smile. "Still. Can't hurt to go out and have a good time while you're here." She gently nudged him in the ribs. "You don't look like the kind of guy who'd turn that down."

He took another sip of beer.

Justin couldn't deny it. Hell, his life had been all about "good times." Tonight, though, watching everyone party, he wondered what it would be like to have more than that. He'd never considered it before, but having something that lasted longer than a few nights or a few weeks or a few months sounded…great.

Since he'd arrived in Miami, Ava appeared everywhere he looked. Starting right after landing at the airport. He'd gotten off the plane and headed toward a woman in the baggage claim who looked like her from behind. When she turned, he reeled with disappointment. Same thing happened with the brunette in the grocery store, and the girl getting on the elevator his first day at work. Each time that he'd realized it wasn't Ava, a little knot had formed in the pit of his stomach.

He'd thought about calling her at least a hundred times to explain what happened, but to say what? *I'm a jerk? I don't make commitments? I feel no responsibility toward anyone, and when it comes down to it, I'll leave the most amazing woman I've ever met the first second I get if that's what's convenient?*

Gee, she'd go for that package in a second, he thought wryly. How could she resist?

Had Ava thought about him since gala night? Or did she hate him and never want to see him again? Option number two seemed more likely.

"Be back in a minute," Chad said, and then turned to make his way through the crowd.

Eden turned her attention to Justin. "I've always wanted to visit L.A. Do you miss it?" she called over the pounding music.

Justin fiddled with his beer glass. Good question. After two weeks in Miami, he'd thought about what he'd left behind every other second. Who he'd left behind.

He'd never been homesick before, but he'd be damned if going home wasn't always on his mind.

"Uh, sure. Has its moments," he replied.

"You from there?"

"I've kinda lived all over, but yeah. I grew up there."

Justin couldn't have been less interested in the cleavage Eden revealed while she leaned forward and sipped her drink, or the legs she revealed with her short shirt.

"You gonna go back when your assignment here ends?"

Justin cleared his throat. "Not yet. But I've got friends and family there, so I can't be away for too long. Just not sure when I'll get a chance to visit."

And after Atlanta, who knew where he'd end up?

Eden finished off her daiquiri and sidled up closer to him. "You are just too cute. You *are* single, right?"

Justin sniffed. "Yeah."

She gave him a playful nudge in the ribs. "How come?"

He laughed, trying to figure out how to answer that. He watched Eden out of the corner of his eye and grinned before taking another sip of beer. "Nobody'll have me."

She burst out laughing. "Yeah, right."

"It's true."

"Sure, it is." Eden giggled and patted his hand. "Don't worry. We won't let you be alone for long." He felt her hand slide up his thigh, where she settled it comfortably, and Justin tried to be subtle about pulling away.

Chad returned and she quickly lifted her hand, and Justin wondered if he'd seen what she'd been up to. From the look on his face, he probably had.

Tough. Wasn't his fault Chad had poor taste in women.

"I'm gonna tell my friend Kari about you. You two would get along great," Eden said, while Chad ordered another round of drinks.

Justin nodded in return, hoping his smile didn't look as fake as it felt. He could be wrong, but from the looks of it, Eden's friends probably wouldn't be his type. He'd recently developed a hopeless attraction to workaholic brunettes with green eyes and incredibly sexy dimples. He had a feeling he'd compare everyone from here on out to her, and it wasn't fair.

"Lets go to Manny's when this place closes," Eden said, glancing from Justin to Chad. "What do you say?"

"Yeah," Chad muttered. "Sounds good."

Under normal circumstances, going to an after hours club would sound great. But tonight, hanging out with a bunch of strangers didn't appeal.

Justin reached in his wallet to pay the bar tab and accidentally pulled out a small, crumpled note stuck to a twenty-dollar bill: *I miss you. Meet me downstairs for dinner at 7.*

When he'd found it stuck to his keyboard one afternoon at Skiv-Ease, he'd grinned from ear to ear and stuffed it in his wallet for safekeeping.

Ava looked so beautiful in the restaurant that night. The simple dinner they'd had was better than any party he'd been to, any trip he'd ever taken. Just hanging out with her, no matter where they were, was the best time he ever had.

One thought kept going through his mind: what would have happened if he'd decided to turn down the position at TimeSpace, take a chance with her, and see where all this led?

Why had he ignored the fact that he'd fallen for her? Maybe because he never wanted to deal with anything that mattered. By the time he figured out that *she'd* mattered more to him than his stupid next assignment, and that leaving had been the biggest mistake of his life, it had been too late.

The night of Charlotte's birthday party, he knew he couldn't lie to himself any more. He couldn't pretend she was just fooling around with him and that it was okay for him to do the same thing. She was the kind of woman who wanted more, and she'd shown him in every way possible she cared about him. What had he done in return? Pretended it didn't matter. He'd ignored his feelings for her, and continued with the plan to take off because he was too scared to do anything else.

Over the past two weeks, he'd been tortured by his big announcement and how much it had hurt Ava when she found out he'd had no intention of telling her he was leaving. She'd spent the final moments of the night she'd worked so hard for with tears all over her face, because of him, and the image haunted him.

When they'd first met, she'd intrigued him. But the plan was to get in and get out, just like always. Falling for her hadn't been part of the equation.

He weighed the options. He could either keep being a coward, or figure out what he had to offer and try and get her back.

The second option. No question.

He stood up, a plan brewing. "I gotta get going."

"What's your hurry?" Chad asked.

"It's early!" Eden said.

"There's something I have to do." He grabbed his wallet and pulled out some money. "I'll catch you both later."

Eden looked at Justin with a look of disbelief while he tossed a few bills on the bar. "Come on, stay a while longer."

"Thanks. I can't."

Justin headed out as fast as he could into the warm, humid night and didn't look back.

"*Are* you sad to be leaving?" Charlotte asked, carrying the last cardboard box from Ava's office. The two of them headed down to the underground garage where Ava's car waited, the trunk full of all the things she'd collected during her Skiv-Ease tenure.

Ava took the box from Charlotte and shoved it further inside the back. "A little, I guess. But there's been so much commotion the past few weeks, I think I'm ready for a little quiet."

"Pretty nuts around here, huh?"

Ava closed the trunk and brushed her hands together. "Yeah. Apparently the Cupid's Beau line tripled profits for the year. And that's only a month later. It hasn't even hit stores yet."

"So the craziness has just started, huh?"

"Guess so." Ava summoned the elevator so they could go back up to the office and grab the remaining boxes. "That's the word around the office. They got an advertising firm to take over, which must have done a good job, because word's all over town. I can't even go get a snack from the break room without people coming up to me and congratulating me. Asking if I can make them special pairs with the slogans that are sold out." She shrugged while the elevator door opened. "Too bad I didn't buy stock in the company. No profit shares for me."

Charlotte put her arm around Ava's shoulder while they strode into the elevator. "Well, what's it like? Having people all over you?"

"Definitely weird."

Charlotte looked her over when they got to her office, probably noticing the lack of a smile...lack of energy...lack of pretty much anything positive right now. "Wait a second. It sounds like you got everything you wanted on gala night. I mean...you *earned* your successes. Aren't you happy about it?"

Ava drew her lower lip into her mouth, wondering what would make her happy right now. Definitely not attention from anyone at Skiv-Ease. "I thought it would mean something to finally get some recognition instead of getting teased all the time, but it's not helping right now."

Not with her sagging, bruised heart.

Charlotte dragged her into her old office. "Well, everyone finally knows that you, my friend, are amazing."

Ava stared at the bare walls and empty shelves. "Everyone but Fielding. Even after gala night, he forbid me to design anything but granny wear.

"What happened?"

Ava took a last look at the mannequins in her office, her only company on more than one night, and grabbed one of the last boxes off her desk. "Monday morning he sent me right back to my Conservo line. And he wouldn't change his mind. Not even at the end of the week when the numbers for Cupid's Beau started rolling in."

"Why?"

"He said they hired someone else with 'more experience' to take over the line. A guy. His *nephew*, to be specific. And he said the Conservo line is where they need me. Bottom line, they used me, and they never intended for me to keep Cupid's Beau. Whether it was a complete failure or a raving success, the results for me would be the same." She managed a grin. "So I told him I was leaving the company."

Charlotte grabbed a box with both hands. "Did he look surprised?"

"Shocked."

"And he just…let you go?"

Ava nodded. "The company's on its feet again. Just goes to show you…"

Charlotte shook her head and frowned while they headed into the hallway. "Just goes to show you that he's an idiot. I was wondering what could have happened to make you quit that job you loved so much."

"It wasn't hard. I'm now completely useless for what he wants me to do, anyway."

Ava thought about the nights she'd stayed up, attempting to play Fielding's game and go back to her Conservo line. She'd tried to figure out how she cranked out girdle after girdle and conservative bra after conservative bra all those years, pleasure pouring through her with every stitch. Now, every bit of the magic had gone.

"I tried, Charl. I really tried to do what Fielding wanted. I *wanted* to go right back to my Conservo line. But every time I sat down to design an oversized bra…or a huge pair of panties…I don't know what came over me. No matter how long I sat there and no matter how hard I tried, I just couldn't do it."

They headed back down to the garage with the last of the boxes.

"If I...tried to design a conservative bra cup, I thought about what kind of sleek material I could use, and how revealing I could make it. Every time I tried to draw a pair of panties, I thought about how it might look better if it rose up here or dipped there. And then when I said 'I'm miserable...hell with it' and let myself do what I wanted, I started drawing some sexy little pairs of panties and tiny little bras. The sexiest things I could possibly think of. I know I don't have anyone to wear them for anymore, but other people do. I thought about how much fun it would be if that were my job...you know, if I could do it full time. Maybe that's what I wanted to do all along, but I didn't think I had it in me." She lowered her eyes and shook her head. "I just think...that's what I'm supposed to be doing."

Charlotte bit her lip. "Sexy stuff, huh?"

"Yeah," she said sheepishly.

"There's no doubt, then. You should go for it."

"I'm going to. I made some contacts at the gala...and I'm starting my own boutique."

They shoved the last of the boxes in the trunk.

"You sure you can do that?" Charlotte asked. "I mean...do you know how?"

Ava shrugged. "It's not a spur-of-the-moment thing. I've thought about doing it for a long time...upscale, hand stitched lingerie, using the finest fabrics, made with love. I've got plenty of money stashed away. Besides, if I pulled off Cupid's Beau, I can pull off anything, right?" She laughed. "I mean...nobody in the *world* thought I could do it in a million years." She pondered for a second, then added, "Well, except for...maybe..."

"Justin?"

Ava gave a reluctant nod.

Charlotte dug her ringing cell out of her purse, and then muttered something before slipping it back in.

"Who's that?" Ava asked, shutting the trunk for the last time.

"Just a...."

Curious, but knowing what the situation was by the tone of her friend's voice, Ava turned and leaned against the car. "A guy?"

Charlotte nodded.

"Well, quit standing there looking guilty, and..." Ava nudged her shoulder. "Answer it!"

Charlotte fiddled with her purse. "He probably wants to go out tonight."

"Great! What are you waiting for?"

"You think I'm going to desert you at a time like this? Leave you alone to wallow in your misery on a Friday night? Your last day on the job?"

"Who's wallowing in misery?" Ava laughed, touched that her friend would pass up a night with a guy for her. She urged Charlotte toward the purse again. "Don't miss out on a date because of me."

Charlotte pleaded with her eyes. "You sure?"

Ava folded her arms across her chest. "Of course I'm sure. Wouldn't you tell me to do the same?"

"Hell, yeah."

"I know you would. So go for it."

Charlotte answered the phone while they climbed into the car.

Not like this was the first Friday night she'd spend alone. She'd spent hundreds of them. Of course, when Justin came along, all that changed. But looking on the bright side, over the past few Friday nights without him, she'd gotten a lot of work done. And who needed a night of rolling around naked with an incredibly gorgeous...and unbelievably sexy guy...when she could get something accomplished for the workweek ahead?

When she got home…alone…Ava decided to unpack her boxes in her home office, and take a break. *So much for accomplishing something.*

She piled her hair on top of her head, undressed, and slid into a warm bubble bath. She'd brought in a bottle of champagne that she'd saved from her birthday last year for a special occasion. She lit some candles, turned on some music, and leaned back against the back of the tub.

The song that Justin stripped to the night of their supposed first date came on her stereo. Grimacing, and remembering how they never made it out of the house that night, she leaned over and switched to the CD feature.

Popping the cork on the champagne bottle, she decided to celebrate the end of an era and the beginning of a new one. For as long as she could remember, Skiv-Ease had been her life. She'd started there a few months after college, and that seemed like a long time ago. She'd been the company joke since her first day on the job, but things were about to change. Had to. They'd have to find someone else to beat up and make fun of from now on. She'd accomplished everything she wanted to, and now it was time to move on and do something for herself. If Cupid's Beau did nothing else, it showed her that.

She believed in her heart that somehow she could get her sexy little underwear business off the ground. Her sexy inspiration would have to come from somewhere.

I'll just have to find a way to do it without him.

Ava flinched, remembering one night in her bathtub with Justin. They'd sat surrounded by bubbles, with her leaning back against his chest. He'd used the opportunity to hide his hands under the water, and let them roam up over her wet hip, across her stomach, and up over her breasts. She'd turned around and he'd kissed her so deeply she melted.

She could deny it all she wanted, but she missed him.

Nobody could make her laugh at a situation the way he did when she felt down. Like the one time Fielding gave her a hard time, but by the time Justin got through with her, she'd cracked up and forgotten all about the lecture she'd gotten. It was one of Justin's gifts...the ability to make someone see an upsetting situation in perspective. By the time he was done with her, the stuff that upset her most felt a little less important.

When she was with him, nothing seemed that bad. She missed his easy-going way with everything and everyone. She missed the way he looked at her like she fascinated him, like he couldn't wait to hear what she said next. Being with him was like being at a party all the time. The most fun party she'd ever been to, even if all they did was hang out on her couch.

She poured herself a full glass of champagne and took a sip.

She missed him waiting in bed for her when she finished her late-night work sessions, how he stayed up for her. She loved the way he held her. And the way he acted like making love to her was the best time he'd ever had.

All a lie, she thought with a grimace. Everything had been a lie. How could she have fooled herself into thinking that one minute they'd spent together meant anything?

She slid deeper under the warm water, thinking that tonight when she got out of the tub, an empty bed awaited her...she'd gotten used to having someone beside her.

I've slept alone most of my life...I can learn to do it again, she thought wryly.

When all the evidence pointed in the opposite direction, how could she have convinced herself that she'd be the one to change him? Why did she think that she'd be the one to make him commit, without any indications he was that kind of guy?

He'd obviously thought of her as a challenge. He'd been the only guy she'd met who'd seen past her very serious suits and her very serious hair and her very serious shoes. Okay, so she was wound a little tightly. She'd been no nonsense right from the start.

She looked like a prude, but he'd suspected something else lay underneath, and his game became to un-prude her. A game to see how long it would take him to charm her out of her conservative panties and get her into bed. And the game continued to see how long he could keep her there. To see how many crazy things he could get her to do with him, and how many orgasms he could get her to have on any given night. And damn it, he'd won his own little game.

And it meant nothing.

He came in and out of jobs, in and out of apartments...and he'd never stay put. Nobody would be enough to make him stick around. His goal in life was to move on, no matter what...or whom...he left behind.

Somehow she doubted he was in Miami mooning over her. It had been a month and he'd probably forgotten all about her.

Face it. He's with another woman tonight.

Some hot, sexy babe he'd met on Miami Beach was probably sinking her claws into him in a hot tub that very minute.

Ava tried to rid her mind of the image of said woman writhing away on top of him.

But she didn't plan on pining for him in her bathtub for long.

The sound of the doorbell startled her, and despite her attempts to ignore whoever was at the door, the ringing continued.

Good timing, she thought wryly, but figured it might be Charlotte in trouble. Maybe her date didn't work out and she needed consoling.

She climbed out of the tub and slipped her robe over her shoulders, and headed toward the door to see who was there.

12

Come on, sweetheart. Open up.

Justin rapped on the front door again and waited for Ava to appear. He hated to wake her if she'd gone to bed, but this couldn't wait.

Standing on her porch, looking at her house, he wondered if she'd want to stay here, or if she'd want him to buy them a bigger place. The idea of living somewhere they picked out together sounded good. But who was he kidding? What did he care what house they lived in? She could pick out whatever house she wanted. And whatever ring, too. He'd buy her ten karats if that's what would make her happy.

Hold on, pal. First you gotta get her back.

He knocked again, thinking he'd lose it if she didn't open the door tonight. Two options: he'd either go insane, or end up like his best friend Jake in high school.

The guy had fallen hard for his girlfriend. When she dumped him for another guy, Jake hardly said a word for weeks. He dropped ten pounds in a month. He gave up on life, despite everyone's best efforts to help him, and spiraled downward. Somebody found him dead a few years later in some motel in Mexico.

Justin swore he'd never end up like his friend, but he wasn't looking too good himself right now.

With a pounding heart, he crammed his hands into the pockets of his jeans and waited for her to answer the door.

For the past five hours on the plane from Miami, he'd tried to figure out what to say to get her back. He'd worked up the guts to tell her what he needed to, and for the first time in his life, he would have to be honest. She knew him too well to accept anything less.

The night of Charlotte's birthday party, everyone warned him that nothing about her was easy. The usual tricks wouldn't cut it. The only way to get her back would be with the pure, unadulterated truth…face to face.

One last rap and the door slowly opened. When Justin saw her face for the first time in a month, it took everything he had not to reach out and pull her into his arms. It killed him that he couldn't. Not yet.

He watched her sexy little mouth fall open. His eyes roamed over her, and he'd never seen a sweeter, more beautiful sight than Ava wrapped in a robe, her hair piled on top of her head. How could he have thought for one second he could leave her? *Idiot.*

"May I come in?" he asked.

"What for?"

Definitely not easy. What did he expect? A warm welcome?

"I need to talk to you. It's important."

After a moment, the shocked look on her face subsided a little and she stepped aside and let him in. She shut the door, leaving them both in total quiet. He glanced around. The living room reminded him of the first time he'd come over to pick her up for their "research trip," and all the incredible times they'd had after that.

Pillows lay right where he remembered them on the couch. The same books sat on the bookshelf, and the same pictures hung on the walls. Everything in the house looked just they way it did a month ago. And he loved everything about it. About her.

Only he sensed that something about her had changed.

She pulled the robe more tightly around her body. "When did you get into town?"

He looked at his watch and gave out a small laugh. "Uh, the plane from Miami landed forty-five minutes ago."

She didn't act like that amused her. "Why'd you come back?"

"I ended my assignment early."

The look on her face told him she was still angry with him. That was all right. He could handle it. At least it meant she cared.

"Ava...this last month I've been more miserable than I've been in my entire life. I didn't want to be in Miami. The job...the city...none of it mattered. Not when all I could think about was what I did to you. I couldn't sleep, I couldn't eat..." He scrubbed one hand over his face.

She paced from one end of the living room to the other. "No need to apologize. It doesn't matter, Justin. I'm not stupid...I'm a big girl and I knew what was going on all along." She turned to him and straightened her shoulders. "A meaningless fling. So you can stop feeling guilty."

He shook his head. "It wasn't a meaningless fling, Ava."

"What would you call it, then? You using me to get a good job performance, with a little Kama Sutra thrown in as an added bonus?"

Was that how she thought he'd looked at it? *Cut her some slack.* Though he'd never thought of it that way, even in the beginning, it probably came off that way when he ditched her. He shook his head.

"That's about all I can think of here, Justin. But hey, I was an easy target, right? Ready and willing..."

He gave out a wry laugh. "Nothing about you is easy." His smile faded and he cleared his throat.

"You got what you wanted out of Skiv-Ease. There's no need to pretend you care about me anymore."

"No pretending about it."

"Oh, please," she scoffed, turning away from him.

"I cared about you right from the start."

"Sure, you did. And you had a funny way of showing it by trying to leave without a word to me."

"I made a mistake. I did what I always do, because I didn't know how to do anything else."

"That is such…"

"I wasn't counting on falling for you, Ava. That was never part of my plan. I didn't know how to handle it. But I did fall for you. Hard."

She watched him with a disgruntled look on her face.

"Ava, I've spent my whole life running from place to place…not knowing where I belonged. All I've done is run."

She furrowed her brow.

"I've never had to work for anything, and I've never stuck with anything…or anyone. Maybe you don't think I paid attention, but since the minute we met, I've watched every move you made. And you amaze me. You're not afraid to commit. And when you do, you give it a hundred and fifty percent. And you don't give up. All those nights you doubted yourself, but you stayed up working on that project, anyway…do you think I didn't notice?"

She folded her arms across her chest and turned away. Maybe he needed to try another tactic.

"It wouldn't have mattered if gala night had been a disaster. It was the process that mattered, not the result, wasn't it? You knew that the commitment would be its own reward, no matter how that night turned out. I've watched it pay off for you, and you've earned everything you have. It's one of the many things I love about you, and now I want to do the same thing. It took a trip to Miami to realize that I'd left behind the best thing that ever happened to me. The only place I want to be is right here with you. I want to commit to you. Maybe you think I can't do it, but I've already made up my mind."

She looked up at him with an uncertain frown and a little sniffle. Was he making progress? He couldn't be sure, but he sure as hell wasn't about to give up now.

"I'm saying I want to be with you, and I'll do whatever it takes to make it work. I can't be without you again." He searched her face, his eyes pleading with hers. "We're good together, aren't we?"

"We were."

"The best. I've never had what we had…with anyone. And I know I never will again."

No turning back now.

He drew in a deep breath, ready to be more vulnerable than he ever had. None of it mattered. Not if it meant he had a chance with her.

"I can't imagine my life without you. I don't want to." When his eyes finally met hers, he knew he had to do this. He wondered if she could hear his heart pounding. "I want to marry you, Ava."

That shocked looked came over her face again. Her lips parted like she was about to speak, but she closed them again.

"I want to spend every day and every night with you for the rest of my life. I want to do anything and everything I can to make you happy."

She stood there, not moving. Then she slowly shook her head, her eyes filled with tears. She sank down onto the couch.

"It took a trip cross-country to realize what an idiot I'd been. But I figured it out. The only place I want to be is with you."

He sat down on the chair in front of her, trying to figure out what that expression on her face meant.

After a moment of pure torture she softly replied, "I don't know how I feel about you anymore, Justin."

His heart sank. "The last thing I ever wanted to do was hurt you. I'll do whatever it takes to make it up to you."

Her eyes met his. "How can I trust you're not going to go away again?"

He shook his head. "I promise you, from here on out I'm not going anywhere without you."

She slowly licked her lips, her brow still furrowed, as if thinking all this over. "I think I just…I need some time, Justin," she said quietly. "I mean, until this second I thought you were gone for good."

"You wrote me off, huh?"

"You didn't leave me much of a choice."

"I know. But I swear to you it's gonna be different from here on out." He tried to muster up a smile before he headed for the door. "I'm staying at the Lowry in Santa Monica…for now, anyway…" He paused. It was all he could do not to pull her into his arms and devour every inch of her. But he couldn't. Not until she came to him ready and willing. "Guess I…I won't take up anymore of your time."

He ached to kiss her, touch her…anything. But she sat huddled alone on the couch, her arms still folded across her chest.

Did he have to leave things like this? But while he headed out the door, it didn't seem like he had much choice. For now. One look at her and he knew this couldn't be the end of his efforts. Could he really let her go before he knew he'd done everything he could?

It's the process that matters, right? As long as he'd made the commitment to making it right with her, the outcome didn't matter.

Yeah, right.

Ava watched Justin climb into his rental car. He looked lost and forlorn, and if that didn't tear her heart out, she didn't know what would.

It took everything in her not to be sucked under his spell tonight. She reminded herself over and over not to reach out to him. Not to throw her arms around him. *Not to beg him to stay.* She never could resist the guy, and no matter how furious at him she'd been since gala night, she wasn't sure what would happen if she touched him. He looked so miserable, and they were sure to end up in her bed, with her comforting him all night. That's exactly what he'd do for her if she needed him to…he'd always been good at that.

And why would she go to bed with him? A special present for breaking her heart? As a reward for him leaving her?

After his car had disappeared down the street, she let the curtain drop and headed for the bedroom. Not that she planned on getting a lot of sleep. Justin had just thrown all of her future plans into turmoil.

She turned from the window and headed for the bedroom, then crawled under the covers and turned out the light. She stared up at the ceiling.

Looking back, he'd always accepted her the way she was, and he'd been rooting for her all the way, since day one, without question. He'd never doubted for a second that she could pull off Cupid's Beau. He'd shown her she could do what she never thought she could, and she owed him for gala night. The night that showed her she was capable of so much more than she'd thought. Because of him, she'd gained a whole new confidence, and she'd quit caring so much about what everyone else thought. *Except for him.*

Rolling onto her side, she tried to get comfortable, but ended up tossing from one side of the bed to the other.

How could she deny that she cared about him? How could she pretend that she hadn't thought about him every second since he'd left? A huge part of her had been missing when he went away.

When they were together, she'd hoped his feelings for her were as strong as hers for him, but she'd never allowed herself to think they had any future together. She'd spent so much time thinking she wasn't good enough for him...not good enough for anyone. But now she knew it wasn't true. He'd shown her a whole other side of herself. She was successful and fun, and he'd made her think that any guy would be lucky to have her.

With a frustrated sigh, she tossed the covers aside and headed into the kitchen to make herself some tea. *Sleepy* time tea.

She put a teabag in a cup of hot water and sat down at the kitchen table.

Deep down, in the back of her mind, she'd known that any future she imagined was only a fantasy. She knew the difference between fantasy and reality, and the reality was that he'd leave her again. It was inevitable. He'd done exactly what she feared he would. But then he'd come all the way back from Miami to tell her he wanted to be with her.

A pretty powerful message.

She knew from the start they had something special, and couldn't deny how good they were together. He knew it, too.

But did she still want to be with him, after all this? After what he'd done? It was her choice, and she had a big decision to make. She could easily let him go, and they could both get on with their lives. But is that what she wanted?

She slowly sipped her tea, and then headed for the bedroom to try and get some rest. She burrowed under the covers and tried to get warm. Before she could manage to drift off, she ended up bolting up in the bed.

It hit her hard.

She loved Justin. Everything in her told her she wanted to be with him for the rest of her life.

"Hi." Ava stood outside Justin's hotel room at three in the morning, a nervous smile on her face when he opened the door. She knew she must look awful from lack of sleep. But she'd made her decision, and if he'd have her, she'd be his forever.

"Ava," he replied, his eyes bright with worry and anticipation.

She missed that mischievous smile on his face she'd gotten so used to being greeted with.

He stepped aside and motioned her inside the room. "Uh, come on in."

She followed his lead, taking in the sight of the beach beyond the private deck. But the view had nothing on the delectable sight of Justin dressed in a white T-shirt and jeans.

"How are you doing?" she asked.

"Not great," he admitted with a little laugh.

"You weren't asleep?"

He scrubbed one hand over his face and gave out a soft laugh. "I tried, but…it's hard to sleep when I'm crazy with wanting and needing you to let me back into your life."

She let out a breath. The guy sure knew how to make her melt.

She glanced around the room. An unzipped duffel bag lay on the floor, and a few clothes lay carefully on the bed. Her heart sank a little. Was he coming or going? What if he planned to leave again tonight?

"How long are you staying at the hotel?"

He scratched the back of his head, pondering. "Well, I just need a few days to find a place to live, and then I'll get out of here. And I've already got a job lined up, so…"

"How'd you manage that?" Not that it surprised her.

"Skiv-Ease asked for me back. Fielding said the company's in trouble again. And I heard that you're not there to bail them out of their latest financial problems, anymore, so…." He shrugged.

"Then I guess you've heard I quit. I'm starting my own company."

She could have sworn she saw admiration on his face. "Good for you. I knew you could do it."

She eyed a huge bouquet of roses with baby's breath and ferns on the table.

He must have caught her looking. He scratched the back of his neck and she could have sworn she saw him blush. "Uh, yeah…" He cleared this throat. "They were…I was going to bring them to you tonight…didn't know if it was the right time…if you shot me down at your house, I wasn't going to stop there. The plan was to try anything and everything I could to get you to talk to me."

Her heart ached with the sweetness of that and she bit back a little smile. She moved closer. "You're really working for Fielding again?"

He shrugged. "Yeah. For a few months. I figure I'll help them out until I can find something steady." He looked deliberately at her. "Something in town."

"That shouldn't take you long. Everyone loves you…"

He raised one eyebrow. "Everyone?"

She let out a little sigh, trying to hold back her grin. Of course she'd included herself in that admission. How could he think otherwise?

He moved closer, and she could smell the clean scent of his T-shirt. And him. And she wanted to pull him into her arms and claim him as hers and hers alone…forever.

Now or never.

She took a deep breath and turned back to him. "I thought long and hard about what you said, Justin."

He scrubbed one hand across his stubbled chin. "Yeah?"

Was that a nervous look on his face?

"Pretty big offer you made."

"Yeah. Well, when you find the right woman, it's time for a big offer. I meant every word of what I said."

"I don't know what kind of crazy woman would turn down an offer like that," she said. "Especially one who's in love with you."

His shoulders relaxed and a look of sheer relief came over his face.

"You'd think that said woman would come as fast as she could to your hotel room and tell you she wants to be with you for the rest of her life."

She smiled at the startled look on his face, thinking that wasn't an expression she'd soon forget.

She laughed when after a few minutes, he grabbed her powerfully and pulled her into his arms. He held her against his body for a few moments without saying a word, and she felt his lips press against the top of her head while he held her.

Then, eager to touch him after so much time apart, she withdrew from his embrace. Then she kissed him with abandon, thinking she was daring, but she was no match for Justin. He kissed her back, and she melted against him, pressing her body against his. One kiss from him and she knew there was no way they could be apart again.

Her heart felt heavy and full, and she figured any minute now she'd explode with happiness.

She pulled his shirt off, reveling in the feel of his skin under her hands.

They fell onto the bed together. Justin's hands slid up inside her shirt, and she helped him pull it off. He stripped her jeans off, his hands stroking over her bare skin.

"I love these," Justin said, his eyes sparkling while his fingers splayed over her latest creation. Her new Conservo underwear was made of soft, silky fabric, but with a very sexy cut.

Ava grinned, a shiver going through her at the feel of his hands on her. "You're the first to see something from my new collection. I'm hoping it's the best of both worlds. Conservative..."

He leaned down and planted a little kiss on her hip. "But very sexy."

With a huge grin, she asked, "So you like them?"

Justin nodded. "Oh, yeah."

Ava rolled on top of Justin, straddling his thighs. She leaned down and planted kisses along his chest, exploring the smooth skin under the hard muscles. She felt his breath draw in.

"Umm...I missed you so much," she murmured.

Justin caught her around the waist, then rolled her onto her back and pinned her beneath him. "Aw, no you don't. No torturing me like that."

"No?" she teased.

"I don't think I can handle any more torture right now."

He sighed, and she decided she'd go easy on him. *Plenty of time to torture him later.*

He brought his mouth to hers and gave her the sweetest kiss she'd ever gotten. She squirmed with delight under his weight.

"I missed you, too," he said. Then his serious eyes met hers. "I love you, Ava."

She melted with his admission. "Justin…"

"You know that, right?"

She nodded. "You know I do." She leaned up and kissed him. "I love you, too."

She reached for the button on his jeans, anxious to get him naked. Instead, he stood up and stripped them off himself. He turned around.

She examined his boxers. *Marry Me.* She burst into laughter. "Are those…"

"Yeah. I bought a pair." Looking chagrined, he turned and climbed back into bed with her. "If you resisted me much longer I was gonna have to break out the big guns."

Laughing, she crawled on top of him, her breasts rubbing against his chest. She leaned down and pressed her mouth to his with everything she felt in her heart, while he held her and kissed her deeply in return.

"So does this mean that you accept my offer? Will you marry me?"

She nodded. "I'll marry you, Justin."

"Good. Because I didn't know what I was gonna do if you said no."

Planting a kiss in the hollow of his throat, she laughed again.

He sighed and put his hands behind his head. "You know, I did so much work for you that first time you came over to my apartment…I think it's only fair your reciprocated."

With a little grin, she bit her lip. "Oh, no. I don't remember. What did you do?"

"How could you forget?" he asked with a huge grin. "I spent the night showing you my underwear?"

She giggled and buried her face against his chest. "Oh, yeah. Among other things."

He laughed. "Yeah, well, it was hard work. I think it's your turn to model for me this time," he said lazily, his gaze roaming over her.

She planted her chin on his chest and looked up at him. "You want me to model for you?" she asked, trying to sound innocent.

"Oh, yeah."

She stroked one hand along his cheek. "Only for you, Justin."

He raised one eyebrow, one hand roaming over her thigh. "For life?"

"Is that what you want?"

He wrapped his arms around her back. "Yeah."

She laughed before she brought her mouth to his. "For life it is, then."

LaVergne, TN USA
22 February 2010

173879LV00003B/15/P